Black Barbie Presents

F*R*I*E*N*D*S

An Urban Fiction Novel

By: Black Barbie

First Printing: 2021
Author Black Barbie
Black Barbie Presents -Printed in the United States of America
Cover Art: Sunny Giovanni
www.authorblackbarbie.com

Acknowledgments

Dedicated to the many people that I've meet and befriended throughout life.

Black Barbie

The Introduction

"Grab ya Glock if you see Tupac! Hay, call the cops when you see Tupac! Hay!"

Ayseana loudly bellowed out the lyrics to a 2Pac song, as she and her friends loudly sang along with the music that had been blaring from out of her cellphone mini speaker.

It had been late in the evening during the five o'clock commute when Ayseana and her girls were fired upon an already packed Bart train. Seeing that many of the commuters had been returning home from a long day of work, they weren't in the mood, nor were they interested in the girl's loud noise and music.

Ayseana was twelve years old at the time, and she'd been the oldest of her two younger sisters. With her mother always away at work or running the streets, Ayseana had no choice but to chaperone her two younger siblings.

When Ayseana considered herself going out, or thought about going anywhere, she'd always be accompanied by her two younger sisters. Despite Ayseana desperate cries for her mother to arrange for another babysitter, Ayseana's voice had always gone on her mother's dead ears.

"Ayeee!" Taj abruptly yelled out with the lyrics of the music along with Ayseana and their other friends as they enjoyed disturbing the commuters on the Bart train that evening.

Seeing that it had been during the rush hour commute, the Bart patrons had grown irritated with the group of girls. If any of the girls stood out to the commuters on the train that day, it would have specifically been Taj and Ayseana with their disrespectful and defiant behavior.

Just as one of the patriots was about to speak out to the group of girls on behalf of the other commuters, the train suddenly approached the girl's stop.

"Ah, I see yo old bitch ass getting irritated. Fuck you, old bitches." Taj turned around to yell out to the commuters while sticking out her tongue and throwing up the middle finger.

Taj enjoyed disrespecting and irritating adults whenever she had the chance to be outside without adult supervision. Seeing that Taj was the only child of a devoted mother and father, she couldn't wait for the opportunity to get outside and act like an unorthodox idiot.

Taj and Ayseana grew up together seeing that they've always been next-door neighbors. With Ayseana being a people person, and always eager to make new friends. Taj on the other hand had been hard to speak with and self-centered, the complete opposite of her best friend.

With Ayseana being a social butterfly, and the popular one of the two. Taj hadn't been well-liked, seeing that she'd been self-centered, defiant, disrespectful, and rude. If it wasn't for Ayseana, Taj wouldn't have a social life. With Taj remaining focused on her education, and deep into school, Taj hadn't cared if she was disliked by her peers, seeing that she had better things to do.

"Ayseana all you worry about is yo fake ass friends, and boys, you need to concentrate and focus on school. I'm not going to be able to do your homework for you all of my life, you need to focus, stupid!" Taj rudely blurted out to Ayseana while helping her prepare for a math test one day after school.

Seeing that there was a big party planned for all of the popular kids that weekend. Ayseana had no choice but to pass her math exam in order for her mother to even consider.

Although Taj hadn't been personally invited herself, she'd planned on going anyway to accompany her best friend.

"Now You know if you fail this math quiz your mama is not going to let you go to that party this weekend." Taj reminded her best friend while getting up from off of the floor to grasp Ayseana attention.

"Girl leave me the "F" alone and get up out of my face, you want to go to that party just as bad as I do, sooo!" Ayseana reminded Taj while walking over toward Taj's radio to turn on her music all while popping her neck.

"Don't talk to me like that Ayseana, the only way that your dumb ass can go out to that party, is with me! And if you don't pass this math test neither one of us will be going anywhere." Taj calmly reminded her while standing in the center of her bedroom with both of her arms folded with frustration.

"Dang, I was only kidding, you always tripping and acting like somebody's mamma!" Ayseana pouted and said while walking back over towards the pile of schoolwork that had been pilled in the middle of the floor.

That week Taj and Ayseana had done everything that they were told to do by their parents. Seeing that they were both determined to go out that weekend and party with the rest of their friends.

But, with Ayseana being the oldest of two siblings, her mother had also made plans for herself that same weekend.

Just as quickly as Friday had rolled around, Saturday had come even quicker. The girls were outside playing when Ayseana's mother called her into the house with a change of plans.

"Yeah ma." Ayseana yelled back out to her mother while walking through the front door.

"Imma need for you to watch your sisters for me tonight." Her mother told her while walking back towards her bedroom.

Ayseana heart suddenly sunken into her chest, seeing that she previously made plans with Taj and her other friends.

"Mom, what do you mean I have to watch the twins, I have plans for tonight." Ayseana whined out to her mother and said, all while following close behind her begging and pouting about how

she never gets to go anywhere without the twins.

"Girl get yo little ass out of my mother fucking face! You got some mother fucking rent money while you out her making plans. I don't give a fuck what you and Taj have planned for tonight. Matter of fact, let me call up Taj's mother to ask her if she can help you babysit since you think y'all grown enough to make plans." Ayseana mother yelled out at her and said while picking up her cellphone to call up Taj's parents.

Ayseana ran out of the house with a face full of tears seeing that she was no longer able to attend the party that night. She ran over to Taj and her small group of friends to inform them of her sudden bad news and change of plans.

"Ah, let me guess, you can't go out because you gotta babysit." Taj interrupted her and said once she noticed the tears in Ayseana eyes.

Before Ayseana could respond, Taj and their other friends, busted out into a loud laughter right in Ayseana's face, with absolutely no consideration for her tears.

"It's not funny, I hate y'all, and while you laughing Taj you weren't invited to the party no way. That's why nobody likes you,

and your ugly self has to stay home too and help me babysit idiot."
Ayseana yelled out at Taj and her group of friends before
storming back towards her home.

Taj stood at the play structure with the rest of her friends looking dumbfounded in the face.

Seeing that she had to help Ayseana babysit, and she wasn't invited to the party with all of the other popular kids. Taj also wanted to cry and burst out into tears, instead, she held tight onto her game face.

"Imma see y'all later." Taj said to her friends while looking
dumbfounded in the face and slowly walking away.

That Saturday when Taj and Ayseana babysat the twins, they hung out on the front porch of Ayseana's house late into the night sitting and looking around their neighborhood. The sun had been hidden by the moon, as the two girls sat on the front porch observing everything around them.

"I wonder who that is moving in the new house across the
streets." Taj said to Ayseana while spitting out the shell of a
sunflower seed and pointing.
Seeing that the new neighbors had been moving directly

across the small street from the girls, Taj and Ayseana noticed a group of kids helping them.

"I wonder if those are their kids helping them." Ayseana *softly asked Taj while taking a high interest in the young boys.*

Suddenly both of the girls had taken a keen interest in their new neighbors.

Taj looked over at Ayseana rolling her eyes, seeing that she had already known why Ayseana suddenly started asking her questions.

The girls continued sitting on the porch past midnight seeing that they were being entertained. Taj and Ayseana had both started wondering amongst themselves why the new neighbors decided on moving in so late at night. Before the girls had looked up and noticed, Ayseana mother had been slowly pulling up the street.

"What in the fuck are y'all fast asses still doing outside at two in the mother fucking morning." Ayseana mother had yelled out at both of them from her driver's window while quickly swooping into the driveway and hopping out of her car.
Without either Ayseana or Taj saying another word to

one another, they immediately jumped from up off of the front porch and ran inside of the house.

"Don't mother fucking run now, keep sitting y'all little fast asses right there." Ayseana mother yelling out loud at them while stomping up the few steps and into the house.

Ayseana and Taj had been standing in the middle of the living room floor impatiently waiting on Ayseana mom to walk through the front door.

"Mamma hurry up and close the door," Ayseana yelled out to her mother while beckoning for her to come inside, once she had noticed her approaching the front door.

Seeing that Ayseana's mom had been in her mid-thirties and full of life, she had always been up for the gossip and bullshit, even if it had come from her kids.

Ayseana mom was different from most parents, and she had been the type to engage in her daughter's mischievous bullshit. Seeing that she was adamant about having Ayseana close to her as a friend.

"I no whatever in the fuck you about to tell me, better be

good! Specifically with you still sitting outside on the front porch at two in the morning." Ayseana mother had said to her while getting comfortable on the couch and taking off her high heel shoes.

Ayseana, Taj, and her mother had sat up for another hour gossiping about the new neighbors and peeking out of the window.

Seeing that Ayseana had brought it to her mother's attention about the neighbors moving in late at night, Ayseana had insisted on her mother giving her answers right then and there.

"Mom why they moving in so late, you can't see much at night." Ayseana had questioned her mother while taking a bite of her late-night snack.

"I'd be scared to move into a new house at night, somebody might be hiding in there." Taj had blurted out and said after Ayseana.

Without Ayseana mother saying another word to either one of them, they had both noticed that it was now time for them to go to bed.

"Y'all little asses get up out of them peoples got damn business. They probably squatters or some shit." Ayseana mother had blurted out and said to the both of them while walking into her bedroom to prepare herself for bed.

"Squatters, what the fuck is a squatter?" Ayseana had looked at Taj and asked while getting into bed.

The weekend had flown by, and so had the time. Ayseana and Taj had now grown close to their once new neighbors, settling their friendships.

Once the girls had grown comfortable with their new neighbors. They learned over time that they moved in late at night due to their parent's work schedules on the weekend.

With the girls learning that their new neighbors had now been the new homeowners of their home, they figured that I wouldn't make a difference about the time of day or night that they had chosen to move in.

The new neighbors had five children, two boys, and three girls. One of the girls where small, around the same age as Ayseana two younger twin sisters. With this being said, Dawn, and Dena were Ayseana and Taj's new best friends.

During their sophomore year of high school, Taj out of all people had popped up with a new friend to complete their crew. At first, Ayseana had grown jealous of Taj new found friend, seeing that she had started getting all of the attention from most of the boys at school.

"I swear to god that this bitch Taj only hanging out with that little black ass bitch just to make me mad." Ayseana had blurted out to Dawn and Dena while walking home from school late one spring evening.

Dawn and Dena had walked in silence alongside Ayseana while Ayseana ranted and raved about Taj and her newfound friend. Neither Dena nor Dawn butted in and said a word to Ayseana. Instead, they silently listened to Ayseana go on and on about a bunch of nothing.

"Oww, y'all bitches act like y'all ain't feeling me right now. Come on now y'all help me, I'm about to lose my mother fucking best friend." Ayseana yelled out to both Dawn and Dena while hopping and jumping around in front of them as if she was a hyperactive two-year-old kid.

"Girl calm down, you out here overreacting." Dawn had

said to Ayseana while softly hitting her on the shoulder with her free hand.

Before Ayseana could get a word in, Dena had chimed in right behind her sister Dawn.

You're overreacting Seana, it ain't even all that serious, you could consider giving her a chance. It ain't like Taj ain't tried to invite her in our circle and introduce her to us as her best friends." Dena had softly said while looking down at the ground and slowly kicking at her feet in the air.

Ayseana had smacked her lips while rolling her eyes at what Dena had just said. Ayseana had hated the fact that Dena would always play the peacemaker. Seeing that Dena had always been quick to avoid any type of conflict or disagreement.

"Look Ayseana, I'm not trying to tell you what to do, all I'm trying to say is that I know you miss your best friend. Hell, I even miss her, but I say that to say this. You have to befriend your best friends, friends for the both of you to grow old. together" Dena explained to Ayseana while preparing to walk inside of her house.

"Think about it Seana, it ain't like you doing something

wrong by introducing yourself to Taj's new friend. The right way Seana, don't go introducing yourself all rude and ignorant." Dena had reminded her while walking through her front door.

Senior year had been memorable for all five of the girls, seeing that they were all able to lean on each other for some type of support. Of course, Taj had graduated top of her class, with all of her friends following close behind.

The group of girls had grown dedicated, determined, and loyal towards their friendship, along with Dena's enforcement for trust and commitment.

Although Amina had only been with the girls for two years throughout high school. She had been just as dedicated to their friendship same as the rest of the crew. If it hadn't been for Taj, Amina would not have graduated from high school.

Once Amina had received her diploma, she hadn't wished on going to college with the rest of her friends. Instead, Amina insisted on hustling and dedicating her support to her four best friends.

Although Dawn and Ayseana had started in college, only Taj and Dena ended up graduating. With Taj receiving her

Bachelors and Masters degree in criminal law and administrative justice. Taj had grown up to be head of her team, with Dena following close behind.

Seeing that Dena had been undecided on her major throughout most of her college years. She had finally received her Bachelor's and Masters's degree in forensic science, taking lead at the opposite end of Taj.

With Dawn and Ayseana dropping out of college and making their main focus men, neither one of them had gone further with their careers.

With Dawn working for Dena as a front Desk Receptionist for the past three years. Ayseana on the other hand played Taj's assistant.

Ayseana had only signed up for the role of Taj personal assistant due to her being able to accompany Taj during her courtroom appearances. Ayseana had wanted to be seen, and on top of that, she wanted to be the first one to have all of the tea in someone else business.

When Taj started her law career fresh out of college, Ayseana damn near got her banned from her practice. If

Ayseana saw your case in court, so had everyone and anyone else in the world who'd been willing to listen to her talk and gossip.

Although the girls had now grown into women, they hadn't grown apart. With Taj being supportive of her group of friends. Everyone on the girl's team was always able to confide in Taj. If it wasn't for financial support, or guidance, Taj had grown up to become someone that her friends and family could always depend on during their toughest time of need.

Although Amina hadn't worked for either Taj or Dena, Amina had known that she had one of the best criminal defense attorneys in the palm of her hands.

With Amina in the streets hustling, she'd been well aware of the risk that she'd been taking. But with her best friend as her lawyer, hustling had always been a risk that Amina was willing to take.

With all five of the girls growing up to be productive adults at the start of their life. Life wouldn't seem right, nor would it be fulfilling without obstacles and hurdles tumbling along to test the girl's faith, loyalty, friendship, trust, and pride.

Although Taj made it big throughout the judicial system, she managed to still live in the hood. It never once dawned on Taj that she lived amongst the criminals and thieves that she often convicted.

Although the girl's lives had seemed as though it would go perfectly planned. It would only be a matter of time before life itself introduced its vowed hurtle to a friendship so closely and tightly knit.

It Gets Complicated

"You know what you can do right?" Taj rudely questioned Ayseana while screaming directly in her face.

Taj and Ayseana had been in the middle of a heated argument since earlier that morning. Just as Taj was preparing herself for work, she had received a call from one of the members of her law association.

"Ayseana, when I had first taken this job ten years ago, you had damn near got me kicked off of the bar and banned from any legal practices. Ah, aht, aht, bitch don't you dare say a mother fucking word. I've listened to yo misguide me for damn near thirty-five years, and I refuse on letting you ruin me!" Taj screamed at Ayseana fuming mad with anger and rage in her face.

Ayseana didn't know how to respond to Taj's reaction, seeing that she had warned her on numerous occasions about gossiping with other people about her criminal cases.

Although Taj had often overlooked Ayseana slick comments and smerkish advances. Taj couldn't have guessed in a million years that her best friend, slash sister could do her dirty knowing the circumstances of her career.

Ayseana, you gotta go! I can't have you here living with me right now, I'm sorry bitch, but I just can't trust you anymore!" Taj had sternly told her with a look of hurt on her face.

"Alright, that's a bet." Ayseana rudely replied without first thinking while swiftly walking away.

After their exhausting argument that morning, Taj had gone to her room, to email the court.

"Blam." was the sound of Ayseana slamming the front door, as she was making her exit to leave Taj house that morning.

Taj's feelings had been hurt, seeing that she had to throw out her sister slash best friend Ayseana.

That afternoon when Ayseana had left Taj house, Ayseana was thirty-two years old. With nowhere to go, and no one to depend on. The clothes on her back and the few things that she had packed up in her used nineteen ninety-nine Toyota Camry, was all that she had owned.

Ayseana had known better than to return home to the comfort of her mother, seeing that her mother always reminded her that she would never amount to anything, nor would she ever be shit.

With this being said, Ayseana had no one else to call on but Dawn.

"Ugh, I'd be damned if I call that black ass bitch Amina, she ain't gone do shit, but tell Taj every mother fucking thing that I said. Besides, that's Taj's mother fucking friend." Ayseana reminded herself while circling Dawn's apartment complex searching for a place to park.

"Oh my mother fucking god, it's never nowhere to fucking park at around here. Ayseana yelled out to no one in particular while waiting on someone to pull away from the curb so that she could take their spot.

Once Ayseana had finally gotten situated in her parking space, she was undecided on bringing in all of her things. Seeing that she hadn't called Dawn at all that afternoon, she had decided with herself that she'd leave the few things that she'd tagged along locked up inside of her car.

Ayseana had always acted dumbfounded towards the activity that had gone on around the hood that Dawn lived in. She often made some of the stupidest decisions whenever she hadn't been guided by Taj.

"Okay bitch, what y'all cooking up in here, I see you got it smelling hella good and shit." Ayseana blurted out to Dawn as she greeted her at the front door, while casually letting herself in.

"Bitch what the fuck you doing over here at this time of day, and why in the hell you ain't at work?" Dawn questioned her while walking over towards Ayseana direction with a bottle of Hennessy in her hand.

"Bitch first off, who in the fuck all up in here. You know you always got a house full of niggas, and badass kids." Ayseana had looked at Dawn and said seriously with a blank expression upon her face.

Before Dawn could respond to Ayseana questions, she had blurted out laughing at what Ayseana had just said.

"Bitch you got me fucked up." Dawn had said through her laughter while taking a puff of her cigarette.

Dawn had informed Ayseana, that she had been at home alone that evening. She had also told Ayseana that her son had been at school, and her baby daddy had been in court for what had seemed like the fifteenth time that week.

"Err, bitch run that back to me again. Now I know that you over exaggerating and shit about the time that he's been to court this week. But bitch, what mother fucking case yo baby daddy out here fighting this mother fucking week." Ayseana had eagerly questioned Dawn while getting up from the kitchen table to get a glass to pour herself a cup of juice to mix with her Hennessy.

"Bitch, you a mother fucking fool, drinking that strong ass shit straight to the neck." Ayseana had said to Dawn while joining her back at the table to pour herself up a shot of Hennessy.

Dawn had filled Ayseana in on just about any and everything that had been going on with her baby daddy. Damn near making Ayseana forget the real reason that she had come over to Dawn's house in the first place.

Ayseana's problems throughout her life had been her concentration and focus. Seeing that Ayseana had focused on everyone else business instead of her own, she continuously lost her focus.

Ayseana seemed to always keep the male's attention, and she always kept an abundance of male friends and attractions. Despite all of the attention that Ayseana has been receiving from various men. She never had the opportunity of having a serious or committed relationship and companionship with any of her male attractions.

"Girl, you better pray to God that Taj is the DA on your baby daddy's case! I don't know what you're going to mother fucking do with that stupid ass nigga." Ayseana had slurred out her words and rudely said to Dawn while now leaning across the kitchen table, tipsy from her mixture of Hennessy and Koolaid.

"Taj." Ayseana abruptly jumped up and yelled as if she had been hit by a bus."

Seeing that Ayseana simultaneously blurted out Taj's name, Dawn had looked at her as if she'd went crazy.

"Bitch are you okay?" Dawn questioned her while lighting up another one of her cigarettes.

Before Dawn could get another question in, Ayseana jumped up into a rant and rave, all while having a fidgeting fit.

Before Dawn had noticed it, she had caught herself slowly following Ayseana's movement as if she was a deranged lunatic.

"Um, okay bitch. I take it that your not oh mother fucking kay." Dawn slowly said to her all while butting out her cigarette and shaking her head at Ayseana's crazy behavior.

Dawn had grown used to Ayseana's bipolar deranged fits over the years, seeing that she frequently and often had them.

"Know bitch for real, you not finna believe this here bullshit Dawn. This bitch threw me out this morning, and it was early and cold-ass fuck might I add." Ayseana sincerely said to Dawn while continuing to lean across the kitchen table drunkenly begging for Dawn's sympathy, pity, and understanding.

Before Dawn could respond to anything that Ayseana just said. She busted out into a loud laughter directly in Ayseana face.

"Wooo bitch, I'm sorry, but this here is some funny ass

shit." Dawn muttered out through her laughter and said.

"Woo bitch, wait until I call up Amina and Dena to tell them about this. I can't wait to hear what Taj about to mother fucking say. Ayseana, who in the fuck do you think that your fooling! If Taj had thrown your black ass out early this morning in the freezing cold as you claim, then there just has to be a good ass mother fucking excuse. Period." Dawn coldly told her while shrugging up her shoulders and reaching across the kitchen table to pick up her cellphone and do exactly what she had just said.

Ayseana was pissed at the fact that Dawn found things funny before she had the chance to explain her side of the story.

"Fuck you bitch, you always quick to take that bitch Taj side and claim that a mother fucker lying to you bum ass bitches or crazy! Fuck you Dawn!" Ayseana boldly yelled out at her, while throwing a slice of bread directly at her forehead while stomping around inside of Dawn's apartment.

Dawn shook her head at Ayseana while she continued to laugh at her as she pouted on her way into Dawn's son's room, slamming the door close behind her as if she was ten.

"Hump, this bitch so mother fucking childish, let me hit up

Amina and tell her how childish this bitch is," Dawn said to herself while picking her phone back up to do exactly what she had been anticipating.

Dawn and Amina had sat on the phone for thirty minutes or more before deciding on three-way calling Taj.

Seeing that Dawn and Amina had enough of guessing and assuming what had really happened between Taj and Ayseana, earlier that morning. Dawn decided on making executive decisions while merging her call-in.

The trio had sat on the phone until late in the afternoon gossiping about Ayseana and what she had done to Taj.

"That bitch staying with you." Amina had chuckled and said to her friends, while also being serious about what she had asked.

"Man, y'all bitches wrong as fuck, what in the fuck am I supposed to do with this crazy ass bitch. I damn near don't got enough room in this mother fucker for all of us that's already living in this little ass son of a bitch." Dawn explained to her friends over the phone, while getting up from the kitchen table to check on Ayseana who had been silent in her son's room.

"Seana, yo ass alright, you old cry baby ass bitch." Dawn playfully asked her while roughly shaking her shoulders to wake her up.

Seeing that Ayseana had a low alcohol intake, but loved to drink liquor. Once her taste buds received a taste of alcohol on her tongue, she'd be sloppy drunk.

When Ayseana took her first double shot of Hennessy earlier that day straight, with a mixture of kool-aid. Ayseana had already been out of her body, mind, and pissy drunk all while easily reaching her limit.

Taj and Amina continued to laugh on the other end of the phone, seeing that they could hear Dawn in the background trying her best to get Ayseana's attention.

"Man, let me call y'all bitches back, this bitch is stone-cold knocked the fuck out, and I'm having a hard time waking this dumb ass bitch up." Dawn explained to her girls over the phone before disconnecting their call and placing her phone in between her bra and breast area.

Dawn had scuffled with Ayseana for another twenty minutes before Ayseana had finally decided on waking up. Soon as Ayseana opened her eyes, and took one look at Dawn, she stared at Dawn as if she was a stranger acting weird.

"Bitch are you okay, and why in the fuck are you looking at me like I'm mother fucking crazy and shit." Dawn had looked at Ayseana and asked, all while yelling in her face and holding both of Ayseana's shoulders to help keep her balance at attention.

"Did you bring a change of clothes with you, Seana, you reek like fucking Hennessy." Dawn questioned her, while now smelling the liquor that had been pouring through her pours.

Ayseana looked at Dawn as if she hadn't said a thing, her head was swimming, and her vision was blurry. Her mind was unbalanced, and she was unable to control her thoughts or her way of thinking.

Ayseana couldn't grasp onto a single word that Dawn had been saying to her, nor could she understand a single word.

"Oh my god Seana, why in the fuck would you come over here and get drunk like this. It ain't even like Taj put you out for no reason. You talk too damn much, you shouldn't be going around telling that girl's mother fucking business, especially when it comes to her job." Dawn reminded her while trying her

best to help Ayseana get up from off of the floor and into the small twin bed.

Every time Ayseana heard Taj's name, she went into a hysterical fit.

"See bitch we not about to do this old bipolar, crazy-ass shit again. It ain't like yo stupid ass got somewhere else to go! You always in somebody else mother fucking business. Girl, you need to get your mother fucking shit together, your thirty-two years old Ayseana. Yo mamma want even let you live with her because you always in somebody's mother fucking business. You need to get your own life together while you out here focused on everyone else!" Dawn scolded her and said while walking out of her son's bedroom and closing the door shut behind her.

Ayseana didn't care, nor had she understood or comprehended a word that Dawn had been saying. Although Dawn was trying her best to lace Ayseana with the realities of her life, Ayseana hadn't responded, nor had she listened to a thing.

Ayseana sat in Dawn's son's room for another twenty minutes before deciding on getting out of bed and stumbling into the living room.

Dawn had now been sitting in the living-room with Amina and a few of their other associated friends when Ayseana had decided on staggering in to make her grand entrance.

"What up y'all." Ayseana sarcastically asked the group of women all while slurring her words and leaning up against the door frame of the hallway wall.

Amina turned to look at Ayseana as if she'd seen a ghost. Once Ayseana noticed Amina's glance, the expression on Ayseana face explained it all.

"Boo bitch! What in the fuck yo black funny-looking ass looking at in the first place? You delusional misguided ass bitch!" Ayseana coldly told Amina, while staring at her harshly and giving her the middle finger while sticking her tongue out at Amina as if she'd been a five-year-old kid.

"Bitch please, you so mother fucking childish." Amina reminded Ayseana while turning around in her seat to continue puffing on her blunt.

Unbeknownst to Ayseana, everyone in the small living-room had already known about what went on between her and Taj earlier that morning. Even though Ayseana tried her best to be secretive about the situation when she confided in Dawn.

Seeing that Ayseana has always been the one to seek the attention of others, she somehow always felt the urge to put on an unwanted show.

"Soo, Dawn, you're going to sit up here and act like you don't hear me or see me over here trying to grasp your attention and speak to you." Ayseana rudely asked her, while now standing between the kitchen and living room of Dawn's apartment with both of her arms folded.

For absolutely no reason at all, Ayseana felt the urge to act out and demand the direct attention of Dawn, Amina, and their few friends. Ayseana was a ball of drama wherever she went, and right now she wants the sympathy and self-pity of her two closest friends.

Dawn, and Amina along with a few of their other friends paid Ayseana absolutely no attention. Seeing that Amina and Dawn had known that Ayseana was good for intentionally starting trouble, both of the women decided on intentionally decided on giving Ayseana no attention at all.

"Look Dawn, I just wanted to ask you if I could bring some of my shit up in here! Don't worry, I'm not asking if I could stay, I'd just like to be able to keep all of my things in one particular place." Ayseana softly asked Dawn, now changing her tone of voice and holding her head down low in desperate search of a pity party.

Dawn hunched her shoulders up and down at Ayseana, indicating that she didn't care if Ayseana brought her things into the apartment or not. Without Ayseana saying another word to Dawn or Amina, she walked out of the front door, to do the exact opposite of what she asked.

Ayseana knew that she wasn't going to bring her things back inside of Dawn's apartment. Instead, Ayseana had already made up her mind.

At first, Ayseana couldn't remember where she'd parked her car, seeing that she was now hungover and drunk from earlier that morning with a faded memory.

"Oh my fucking gosh, my dumb ass can't remember if I parked in the damn complex, or outside on the fucking streets. At

*times like this, I wish that I had a newer car with a key alarm."
Ayseana complained to herself while walking around the small
apartment complex checking the visitor's parking stalls.*

Ayseana stood outside of Dawn's apartments for more
than forty minutes walking up and down the street trying her
best to remember where she last parked. Before she'd come to
realize that she parked on the opposite side of the street.

Once Ayseana made it across the busy intersection of
Bancroft, she quickly noticed that something looked strange
with her car. Once she approached her car, she'd come to notice
that her side passenger window had been biped. Not only had
her side window been biped, but to add further insult to injury,
the few things that she owned had been missing.

Ayseana's car may have been considered as a mobby to
others, however, to Ayseana it was a car that she worked hard
for, and to her it meant everything.

Seeing that Ayseana's vehicle registration and liability
insurance had been in Taj's name, Ayseana didn't feel the need
to report the incident to her insurance or the authorities.

The last thing that Ayseana wanted to do that evening,

was to go back inside Dawn's apartment and fill her and Amina in on what just happened.

Ayseana had been having a bad day since the start of her morning. The last thing that she needed was to hear her so-called friends talk down on her during her vulnerable stage.

Instead, Ayseana wallowed in her self-pride as she whipped the chipped glass pieces from the front passenger seat of her car and cried her way to the nearest Motel 6.

"Hay Dena, what you been up to lately, I sure haven't heard from you in a few days." Taj confronted her over the phone while fidgeting around with a few papers at her desk.

Dena hadn't known about what went on with Taj and Ayseana earlier that week. Seeing that Dawn didn't want to hear Dena's mouth about what happened between Ayseana and Taj. Dawn purposely avoided the conversation with her sister.

"Nothing much girl, you know how it is, working, trying to make a living." Dena softly replied to Taj while mixing a few chemicals inside of a small beaker.

Taj had been at her desk, fumbling through a few papers

while she filled Dena in over the phone. Dena on the other hand had also been at work working on various forensic cases.

The two women sat on the phone for more than two hours, going over various case files and lab test results. Seeing that both of the women had been intrigued and focused on their upcoming cases, Taj had overlooked the drama with her and Ayseana and decided on not filling Dena In.

After speaking with Dena briefly about work, Taj decided then that Dena was focused and didn't need to hear about any drama on her and Ayseana's end.

"Now you know that I'm usually not the one to complain, however, I'm really getting tired of my sister and her nigga and his criminal cases." Dena surprisingly blurted out to Taj over the phone while they briefly sat in silence.

Seeing that Dena has always been the peacemaker and never the one to complain about anything. Unbeknownst to Dena, she'd now caught Taj's full undivided attention. Taj was a Criminal Lawyer soon preparing to become a District Attorney, she was always prepared to hear about someone else gossip or bullshit.

"Girl, I can just fucking scream, I swear, this shit doesn't make know mother fucking sense to me. I mean, I just don't fucking get it with the way that he keeps going back and forth to jail for the same got damn thing. And on top of that Taj, it seems like the nigga is arrested each and every mother fucking day with absolutely no consideration for either one of our careers. I wonder if Dawn stank ass takes my career into any type of consideration, not even just mine Taj. What about you, what about your career and the dreams that you're reaching towards." Dena questioned Taj with hesitation and concern in her voice over the phone.

Taj hadn't responded to Dena's question seeing that she never consider her career or the consequences that may have come along with what she'd been doing. Instead, Taj sat on the other end of the phone dumbfounded seeing that she's never taken into consideration the outcome of helping her hood with various convictions and criminal cases.

Seeing that Dena had now placed Taj into deep thought, Dena had decided on picking their conversation right back up from where she'd left off.

"Don't you think that one day you'll get a call saying hay

Taj, you've been intentionally stalling or throwing out such and such criminal cases." Dena mimicked in a masculine voice to her over the phone. While now leaning over the counter that she'd been working at looking concerned about what she just mentioned.

Taj had also focused on what Dena had been saying to her over the phone. Seeing that she'd never considered anything.

For all that Taj figured, she was looking out for her people and doing the right thing. Taj never looked at getting herself into any trouble seeing that she'd been her own superior. But at the same time, she hadn't looked at the consequences of a criminal conviction for herself nor Dena.

After Taj and Deana spoke on Dawn for what seemed to be an eternity. Taj decided on briefly filling Dena in on what happened earlier that week between her and Ayseana.

"Personally, I feel as if they all take advantage of everything that we've done and do for all of them. Now, let's also keep in mind, and remember that our family and friends ain't no group of church-going saints." Taj softly told her over the phone

after filling her in.

With Dena now whining to Taj about their small circle of family friends. Taj had begun to deeply think about her future and her career.

Dena had always been the peacemaker, and never the one to nag or complain about anything or anyone. Taj on the other hand had no other choice but to take into consideration every word that Dena said.

Ayseana called herself staying away from everyone, by confiding herself into her own space and delusional dreams.

Ayseana felt as if she'd became a failure, and she'd felt as if she'd given up on herself.

At the age of thirty-two, Ayseana finally comes to realize that she accomplished nothing and that she had nothing.

Instead of Ayseana taking a negative situation and forcing it into a positive one, Ayseana drifted on her past. She conclusively came to notice that if it wasn't for Taj, she wouldn't have looked as if she accomplished the few things that she has done.

That night as Ayseana sat in her motel room, she vowed to herself that moment, that she wouldn't reconnect with her old friends until she had something going for herself.

Ayseana further went on to tell herself that no matter how long it takes, she'll never contact her family and friends until she's satisfied with the way that she's living.

The only thing that Ayseana had known, was that she needed to focus on herself. For thirty-two years, Ayseana finally comes to realize that she's always placed her attention and focus somewhere else.

It had been three weeks since anyone heard from Ayseana, or seen her. After reaching out to Ayseana's mother, Taj comes to learn that her mother and twin sister hadn't heard from her or seen her either. Taj further learned that Ayseana hadn't been in the hood at any of her friend's houses either.

Seeing that Ayseana had always been known for disappearing, it hadn't been strange or unusual for her to occasionally come up missing.

With the fact that Taj had thrown Ayseana out of her house, it was only a matter of time before Taj would hide inside of a shell with pity and unwanted self-guilt.

"Well, you know she'll pop up whenever she feels ready,"
Dawn said to Amina when they had both been in question about
Ayseana whereabouts.

Seeing that Dawn's baby daddy had been fighting a dope case at the same time that Amina had been fighting her own case. Dawn and Amina would regularly accompany each other to court whenever needed.

With Amina and Dawn's baby daddy sharing the same Lawyer, it was no wonder that they always shared the same court dates.

For some strange reason, Amina felt odd that morning, when she normally felt confident when walking into the courthouse.

Seeing that Taj hadn't been keeping Tabs with her on her case as she'd normally done, Amina felt uncomfortable on this particular day.

Dawn noticed the sudden shift in Amina's mood, so she decided on questioning her sudden reactions.

"Whats suddenly gotten into you?" Dawn quietly asked Amina while walking through the metal detector directly behind her, and in front of her baby daddy.

Amina hadn't answered Dawn right away, seeing that she was busy with the deputies waving their handheld metal detectors around her body. Once everyone had been cleared to enter the courthouse, Amina decided on answering Dawn's question.

"Bitch I feel like Taj and Dena been acting funny, and I feel like we bout to get some bad news soon as we walk inside of this here courtroom." Amina anxiously said to Dawn with the assurance of her voice, all while walking as if her hands and feet had been shackled with chains.

Dawn hadn't known how to reply to what Amina just said, seeing that she too felt a bit awkward about attending court that morning as well.

With everything going on between Amina and Dawn's baby daddy criminal cases, Dawn felt that it was best to keep a tight lip. Dawn decided with herself that moment that it was best for her not to respond to a word that Amina just mentioned.

While in court that morning, Taj always kept a stern and strict face with a low profile. She never gave anyone that she may have known attending court recognition.

Seeing that Dawn's baby daddy case had been called up first, Dawn's heart had sunken in once she heard the judge hit the gravel and revoke his bail.

Amina's case had been called upon by the judge next. It seemed as if Taj had a domino effect that morning. Taj had revoked everyone's bail, all while remanding everyone into custody. Damn near every criminal that attended the courtroom that morning had been taken into custody.

The once filled courtroom had been just about empty before noon. With Taj in control of the courtroom and running the show, the bailiffs handcuffed everyone with pending cases, while the judge swiftly revoked their bail.

Seeing that everything happened so vastly, Dawn hadn't known how to react nor how to think. The only thing that Dawn noticed that morning, was that she went home alone, without the company of Amina, or her baby daddy.

With Dawn's attention being driven into a deep trance, she hadn't paid Taj any attention as Taj swiftly walked past her. Taj walked past Dawn so fast that afternoon after court, until Dawn hadn't recognized who Taj was.

Although Dawn hadn't recognized Taj, Taj noticed exactly who Dawn was. This was one of the reasons why Taj had been striding down the hallway swiftly, without ever looking towards Dawn's direction.

Dawn had left the courthouse that afternoon questioning her loyalty, friendship, and faith in Taj.

Far as Dawn was concerned, Taj could of at least explained to her the reason for revoking everyone's bail and remanding them back into custody. Instead, Taj walked directly past Dawn without any recognition, although Dawn hadn't recognized her.

"Friendship! Humph, what in the fuck is that? " Dawn questioned herself while sitting at the intersection of a red light.

Dawn had been returning home from court that afternoon in deep thought and sudden depression. She couldn't help but question herself why Taj's sudden decision.

BLACK BARBIE

"Boy I tell you, we all thought Ayseana was crazy for running off and doing her own thing. These bitches ain't yo mother fucking friends! Now of days hoes just want to be in your face to get up in your business, and mother fucking compete where they don't compare!" Dawn aggressively yelled out to herself while driving down the intersection headed towards the freeway.

After court that week, Dawn refused on reaching out to Taj, seeing that Taj hadn't reached out to her explaining her decisions.

That week had been tough for Dawn, seeing that she'd been humiliated and embarrassed by her so-called best friend. Dawn hadn't known what to think of Taj nor did she know how to react. Seeing that Dawn also hadn't heard a word from her baby daddy or Amina.

If depression had a face, Dawn was the poster image. With Dawn placing the blame for her depression on Taj's decision, Dawn started resenting the sound and thought of Taj's name or appearance.

Dawn had started to feel the same way that Ayseana had

done when she assumed that Amina wasn't their friend back when they were younger. Unbeknownst to anyone, Dawn made herself despise Taj's entire existence.

"Shit, I don't know why me and my sister befriended that fake ass bitch in the first place." Dawn questioned herself one day while chilling at home on her living room sofa inhaling a cigarette.

With Dena out of the loop, and unaware of what had been going on with Dawn's baby daddy case. It started to mentally eat away at Dawn's brain and drive her somewhat insane. With Dawn refusing on speaking with anyone, her isolation picked away at her brain.

Dawn was starting to cause depression on herself, by making her brain rattle with a situation that she couldn't control or maintain. Dawn had been so reckless without the guidance of her baby daddy until she not only isolated herself from the world, but she also avoided any contact with her son.

The only thing that Dawn had been concerned about was the fact that her cellphone or house phone ranged with correctional facility across the caller ID. Seeing that neither phone ranged displaying the caller ID option that she's chose, Dawn sunken deeper into her depressed mood.

If her son needed for his mother to leave the house and attended to his wants and needs. Dawn's son could certainly forget about it, because it wasn't happening, nor was he able to get his mother to move.

Dawn refused on leaving her apartment because she refused on missing her baby daddy's phone call. Although her baby daddy hadn't reached out to her in what seemed to have now been two months.

Meanwhile, Dawn's baby daddy sat in jail assuming the opposite of what Dawn had been thinking. Dawn's baby daddy assumed with himself that Dawn had been in chaos with Taj remanding his bail. Dawn's baby daddy couldn't come to grasp with himself seeing that Taj and Dawn had been such good friends.

With Amina's case being called after his, and with Amina being shipped off towards the opposite side of the jail. Dawn's baby daddy hadn't known what had been going on with Taj or his case that day. The one thing that he did know of for certain, was that he wasn't reaching out to the mother of his only son.

"Man fuck that bitch bra, I don't give a fuck what naan nigga got to say up in here! That bitch set me up with her hoe ass best friend so she can go mother fucking lay up with some old bitch ass nigga. I'm telling y'all main, that bitch don't give a fuck about me." Dawn's baby daddy explained to his celly while laying on the bottom half of the two-man bunk bed.

For once, Dawn didn't have her baby daddy in her or her son's life, nor had she been around any of her family and friends.

Amina had been incarcerated for what seemed like an eternity although it had only been two months.

Far as Dawn's son's father had been concerned, it was all a setup. He insisted on settling with the thought that Dawn set him up, seeing that the assistant DA was his baby mother's best friend.

Dawn's baby daddy had been stressed out of the game, seeing that he had various things running through his head.

With a jailhouse full of fake philosophers, psychologists, and mentors. Dawn's son's father hadn't known what to think of, far as he was concerned, he wasn't reaching out to Dawn for answers.

Dawn's son's father had been so confused as to why he'd been incarcerated until he was for sure with himself that Dawn set him up to be with another man. He'd been so focused on what he assumed Dawn attempted until he completely lost thought of why he'd been incarcerated in the beginning.

Amina on the other hand hadn't been upset with Taj at all for doing what she had to do. Amina had been reaching out to Taj, and Taj had been placing money on her books.

After Amina's arrangement and sentencing, she decided on reaching out to Taj. Amina decided on contacting Taj to ask her what it was that she may have needed to do to lighten up her sentence. Once Taj explained to Amina the importance of her career, Amina had no choice but to respect Taj's decisions.

Amina understood Taj's position as an assistant DA, and she'd also been aware of the risk that she'd been willingly taking when she was out in the streets hustling.

Far as Amina had been concerned, she had a long fair run in the streets. With the assistant DA as her best friend, Amina had known for certain that she could handle any type of sentence that had been thrown in her direction.

Dawn on the other hadn't taken things as lightly as Amina, seeing that she hadn't heard from her son's father since his court date in over four months now. Although Dawn contentiously wrote him trying desperately to reach out to him. Dawn's letters always seemed to have ended up on dead ears, seeing that she never received a response.

With no communication from her son's father within the last four months. Dawn started to feel just as reckless as he'd felt while he was being held behind bars. Unbeknownst to either one of them, they carried the same emotions and feelings. Due to Dawn's baby daddy's stubbornness, he refused on reaching back out to her or making a call.

Although Dena hadn't had any communication with her sister in the past four months. Dena hadn't reached out to Dawn, seeing that she was the reason behind everyone being apprehended in court that day. However, no one implemented Dena within the choices and decisions that Taj made.

Dena felt guilty, and she felt bad about encouraging Taj to revoke everyone's bail in court that morning.

The only signal of peace that Dena had due to her implementation of Taj's decision was the constant communication with Taj and Amina. Although Dawn was her sister by blood. Dena mentally abandoned Dawn out of guilt and confusion about what had taken place in court that morning.

With Dawn now out of the picture, and with Ayseana out somewhere in the world doing her own thing. What once seemed like an unbreakable bond slowly started shedding due to their lack of communication, space, and respect for one another choices and decisions as friends.

Moving Ahead

Ayseana had been out doing her thing when she bumped into her now new male companion. A year before Ayseana hitting rock bottom and leaving behind all of her family and friends, Ayseana found happiness.

Ayseana had now been living in LA, in the Hollywood hills, with her new career and soon-to-be husband. She'd been enjoying her new life, and she refused on reaching out to any of her so-called family and old friends.

Ayseana figured to herself since she'd always came out on the laughing end of the stick she had no reason to inform anyone from her past about her new happiness. Ayseana cut off all tides with anything and everyone associated with her friends and family.

Ayseana figured that she had bigger plans for herself, and she wanted for her new girlfriends to notice her on the big screen as she hosted her morning talk show.

The Morning Gossip Section, to everyone in LA, was huge as an early morning talk show. For the residents of Los Angeles

County, they looked upon Ayseana as somewhat of a big importance.

Ayseana wanted for her family and old friends to see firsthand for themselves that she to had been a successor of their so-called elite family and friendship.

During Ayseana's first-year commitment to her new husband, she never once mentioned to him anything about her family or old friends. The only reason that Ayseana's husband had known the little that he did know about her mother, was because Ayseana insisted on proving a point to her.

Instead of Ayseana properly introducing her mother to her new husband the appropriate way. Ayseana decided on calling her mother to inform her that she now had stability and control of her own life.

Seeing that Ayseana was so high upon her new horse, she forgot where she'd come from. Not only had Ayseana forgotten where she'd come from, but she'd also forgotten to remain humble, seeing that she could easily lose everything that she assumed she owned.

Ayseana had become so cocky and arrogant with herself

and with her carefree. Until she hadn't come to notice her nonchalant ways, Ayseana seemed to have forgotten that the wrath of God could quickly take everything away.

Although Ayseana had been upset with her mother and friends, she quickly forgets about who supported her in the past when she had nothing. Ayseana erased the fact about who supported her during her toughest times throughout her life.

Ayseana easily wrote off her past, by forgetting those that dealt with all of her mishaps that molded her for her now sudden happiness.

One night, while Ayseana had been home alone without the company of her husband, she started thinking to herself. Ayseana suddenly thought of how her life could have been with the acknowledgment of her family and old friends. Ayseana imagined her success with all four of her close friends, as she suddenly regretted the majority of the decisions that she's made.

Ayseana sat in the center of her eighteen hundred square feet living-room enjoying her own company. Which was now something that Ayseana had grown accustomed to.

Seeing that Ayseana became used to her husband's absence, she often found herself daydreaming about the future and her new image.

"I can't lie, this celebrity lifestyle is boring as fuck, I'd do anything right now to be drunk in the hood with my bitches." *Ayseana said out loud to herself while scrolling through a social media app on her cellphone.*

Although Ayseana's social links had been run by her PR team, she never personally had any interest in what had sociably been going on in her life. But, with boardum comes interest, and with interest comes impact and feelings.

At first, Ayseana was hesitant to login into any of her social media sites seeing that the comment section could be cruel and mean.

When Ayseana first logged on to one of her accounts, she started admiring the likes that she'd been receiving. She'd been enjoying the majority of the comments, in the comment section as well.

After enjoying her millions of followers, and thousands of views that she'd received. Ayseana decided to search through her follower's list to see if any of her old friends had been coincidentally following her.

With Ayseana now living the good life and forgetting all about Taj, Dena, Dawn, and Amina. Ayseana came to learn the hard way, that her friends had also forgotten all about her.

Ayseana was shocked once she comes to notice that none of her so-called best friends hadn't been following her on social media.

Ayseana's mind went into a frantic rave once she found out that no one close to her had been supportive of her newly found fame and career.

Not only wasn't any of Ayseana's so-called best friends not following her on social media, but her younger siblings weren't following her as well. To add insult to injury, Ayseana's younger twin sisters also had blocked her from all of their social media accounts. Ayseana's main reason for deciding on logging into social media in the first place was to see if she'd been followed by her family and friends.

The fact that no one deeply rooted in Ayseana's past had been following her on social media, made Ayseana suddenly go crazy. Ayseana went into a tantrum seeing that the people she wanted to notice her the most, hadn't.

Ayseana was baffled and confused with the fact that her friends hadn't been following her, and her siblings had blocked her. Ayseana couldn't understand why no one seemed to have noticed her new fame or seemed desperate to follow her interactions.

Ayseana couldn't come to understand why hadn't her family and friends missed her, searched for her, or looked into seeing how she's been.

That night, Ayseana sat in deep thought for hours depressed and in an unwanted mood. When in reality Ayseana brought all of her loneliness and depression amongst herself.

Once Ayseana decided on forgetting where she came from while abandoning her family and friends. Ayseana failed to realize by deserting the people who once supported her when she had nothing and no one, she'd always feel empty and incomplete.

Ayseana couldn't understand to realize that no one noticed her success, happiness, career, or newfound fame and fortune. The life that Ayseana chose to run off and create for herself, had been fabricated from the start.

Although Ayseana's husband pushed her into focusing on herself and bettering herself into a productive woman. In the end, Ayseana's husband was using her for his own personal security and financial growth.

Ayseana's husband known if he'd pressed up on Ayseana to become better than the woman that she'd been. She'd later mold herself into a woman with a better mindset and vision, her husband had known that he'd be able to later secure a bag in the end.

When Ayseana and her husband first meet, he noticed right away Ayseana insecurities and flaws. Seeing that Ayseana's husband preyed like a vulture on vulnerable women. Unbeknownst to Ayseana, that day at the Motel 6 lobby when she first meet her husband, he'd been the predator, and Ayseana had been the prey.

Ayseana and her husband barely and rarely made any physical contact with each other after her fame and financial wealth bloomed and blossomed.

Ayseana husband could be traveling anywhere in the world with any woman besides his wife. Lord forbid for Ayseana to speak up on her behalf and say anything about his whereabouts.

If Ayseana looked as if she were to open her mouth about his absence or mistreatment, her husband would throw a hissy fit. Ayseana's husband would immediately reverse the situation and throw everything back in her face. He'd accuse Ayseana new career for keeping her busy, and him away, all while reminding Ayseana that she was nothing without him. He'd contentiously mentally abuse Ayseana by reminding her what if he decided on walking away.

Ayseana's husband had her brainwashed, and Ayseana come to recognize that he meet her at a vulnerable time in her life. Ayseana knew deep down inside that she should leave her husband if she wanted to. However, she'd also no that she'd have nowhere to go and no one to turn to, seeing that her new friends weren't really her friends.

Ayseana regretted the way that she turned her back on her friends and family. With the way that she abandoned everyone and disappeared, she felt that she had known choice but to stay and suffer with her husband.

That night, Ayseana sat her phone down on the living room sofa before walking up the stairs to prepare herself for bed. When Ayseana lied down to rest for the night, not only had she been confused, but she'd also went to bed in a depressed mood.

Taj, Dawn, Dena, and Amina all were still tightly knitted, rocking together as if Ayseana never disappeared. The four best friends carried their lives on through thick and thin together as if Ayseana never existed.

Once Dawn calmed herself down and regained self-control with the fact that Taj sentenced her son's father. Things between Taj and Dawn were right back on track as if nothing ever happened between the two of them.

Although Dawn learned the hard way about the loyalty of her son's father, she later eagerly moved onto a new man that everyone considered to be better for her and different.

Once Dawn snapped out of her depression and started getting out again. Dawn ran into her now fiance at the YEP recreation center while picking up her son one day. Dawn had been running late that evening and had been looking a hot mess when she'd finally decided on getting out of bed to pick up her son.

Dawn hopped out of her car vastly as she walked through the parking lot with her head held down low.

Seeing that Dawn had suddenly been in a rush, she'd been fumbling through her purse in search of her house keys when she literally bumped into her now new man.

"Excuse me." Dawn carelessly said to the gentleman while continuing to fumble through her purse as if she hadn't just excused herself while passing.

At first, the gentleman paid Dawn no mind, overlooked her apology until he turned around and noticed her huge apple shape that she carried so delicately around her hips.

At that moment, the gentleman debated with himself while standing outside of his car on waiting for Dawn to come back out of the center or not. The gentleman assumed with himself, that the shape Dawn carried, must have come with a man. He further concluded with himself that she'd also have to have kids seeing that she'd been rushing inside of the reck center.

Dawn made her way towards the front desk to check her son out for the day, while half hardheartedly speaking to the receptionist. Whatever she'd been fumbling for in her purse must have slipped her mind, seeing that she'd now been walking out of the reck center with her head held up high.

Whatever changed Dawn's mood from fumbling through her purse and walking outside with all of her pride as her head was held high; attracted the gentleman's unspoken affection.

"Excuse me miss, I wanted to acknowledge your apology from earlier." The gentleman said to Dawn in a masculine voice while presenting himself to her with his hand extended and winking his right eye at her son.

Dawn's son looked up at his mentor and coach with a huge smile on his face. Seeing that he'd always wished for his coach to have been his father.

Dawn glanced down at her son, to notice the brightness of his smile, before extending her hand back out in a flirtatious matter.

Although it took a while for Dawn to open up to her new man, he'd been patient and honest with her. Without trying or forcing their situation, Dawn and Carl's relationship worked out accordingly without being planned.

Unlike Ayseana, Dawn shared her relationship and newfound happiness with her family and friends, the same way that Carl did. Although many of the double dates that Carl tried setting his friends up with Dena, Taj, and Amina hadn't quite worked out so well. On the other hand, Dawn bumped into her true love at the YEP recreational center.

Once Dawn had been in her relationship with Carl for about a year, she finally decided on loosening up by introducing Carl to her family and friends.

Once everyone was finally able to meet Carl, they enjoyed him for being patient with Dawn during her time of need and depression. Everyone was excited for Dawn and her son seeing that she'd stepped out of her boundaries and decided on dating a different type of man.

With Carl being the businessman that he was, Carl continuously came up with all types of activities and trips for

Dawn and the girls to enjoy together as a group. Carl enjoyed his new family and relationship, he enjoyed making plans for Dawn and her friends, and he enjoyed the fact that he'd been dating a grown woman.

Dena, Dawn, Amina, and Taj always seemed so wrapped up in their lives, that they considered themselves to adult for social media.

The girls agreed as a group earlier on in life that social media was unsafe and explicit of their personal life and well-being. Seeing that Amina always been in the streets, she'd known first hand what bragging and showing off on social media could later bring.

With Taj being an assistant DA, she's seen many cases brought to justice with the tap of a button and the scroll of a finger. If social media hadn't been accumulating them any type of revenue without being noticed or seen, there been no need to entertain, share, tap, or like anyone else business including their own.

Although Dena and Taj never clicked with any of Carl's friends, they enjoyed the various selection of men. It wasn't that

Dena and Taj couldn't find a connection with any of Carl's friends, it was the fact that they chosen not to connect with any of his friends.

Dena and Taj had been undercover freaks, and they enjoyed the attention that they both desperately seek. Seeing that both of the girls had a career that required all of their time if their companion wasn't the DA or a Forensic Pathologist your commitment or companionship didn't stand the time or place for further existence.

Taj and Dena both known their worth when it came to the value of a woman and dating other men. Not only were they both perfectly figured and attractive, but they also had the income that held a lot of heavyweight for both of them. Dena and Taj didn't have to hustle or scam, they had a career, and they both know that it took them years to get where they are.

Dena and Taj knew what they wanted when it came to dating various men, and it hadn't been falling in lust or love with a man who had less than the both of them.

One night while the girls were all out chilling as usual. Unlike most of their girl's nights, they'd go out to the movies, or meet up at a restaurant or bar. However, on this night they'd randomly changed their plans and decided on meeting up at Dena's house instead.

Dena stayed in a nice secluded area, tucked tightly within the Piedmont hills. From the first glare of Dena's immaculate home, you'd tell yourself that she was a huge celebrity, or that she had a large family. Dena had taken pride in her home, and it was immaculate, Dena worked hard for herself, and she knew first hand what she deserved.

Seeing that Dawn, Taj, and Amina decided on carpooling to Dena's house that night, they all arrived together.

"Can you believe how your sister got this here huge ass setup," Taj asked Dawn while looking directly at her from the driver's seat.

Taj leaned over the driver's door to press the intercom and let Dena's security know that they needed to be escorted in.

"You see why I don't let Carl come over here and visit with me, he's going to think that were some rich ass celebrities. And I for one don't want him to be thinking that I've been lying and playing games with him." Dawn replied to Taj while hunching up

both of her shoulders.

"Girl, how in the fuck is Carl going to be mad at you for your sister having money." Amina chimed in and said while tapping Dawn on the shoulder to assure that she heard exactly what she just said.

"Shut yo ass up Amina, you always got some old stupid ass shit to say." Taj said while laughing and shaking her head.

"Well, I'm just saying shit. How in the fuck is he going to get mad when this Dena's shit, hell, she don't get access to her sister's money." Amina replied while stepping out of the car.

Both Taj and Amina had been laughing hysterically while Dawn had been rolling her eyes at the both of them while giving them an evil stare.

"Fuck the both of y'all bitches, hurry the fuck up before I lock you hoes out of my little sister's house." Dawn sarcastically said before running up the huge stairs and through the large double doors.

"Owe, I no this bitch didn't." Taj looked at Amina and said, while quickly running up the stairs after Dawn.

"Psst, please, I wish this bitch would lock me out of her baby sister's mansion, the only thing that this bitch needs to be locking up is her apartment," Amina said to herself, while hysterically laughing and slowly strolling up the stairs.

Once all three of the girls made it inside of Dena's house, Dawn had been yelling and screaming in the foyer hollering out Dena's name. Even though the housekeeper just informed her that she'd go get Dena from out of her office.

Dawn loved the fact that her younger sister had been doing big things, and she made sure that Dena's staff always known when she entered the building.

After a casual conversation, with a lot of chatter and a bunch of laughter, Dena and the girls made their way to her private home theater.

"Okay bitch, I see that somebody done did some rearranging up in here." Taj happily said to Dena once she noticed that Dena rearranged her second master bedroom into a small home theater.

"Why thank you bitch, I mean I do try." Dean playfully replied while kicking up her heels as if she was Betty Boop.

Amina walked around the theater in amazement, while Dawn had been happy to make wedding plans seeing that her younger sister wouldn't mind.

"Owe bitch, let me and Carl have our wedding here." Dawn gracefully blurted out with a huge smile upon her face bright as her eyes.

"I thought that you didn't want for Carl to come over to your baby sister's house." Amina blurted in and said.

Taj looked over at Dena as she busted out laughing, as Dena looked confused about what had been just said.

"Why wouldn't you want for Carl to come over Dawn." Dena questioned her older sister as if she was whining in recognition of what Amina just said.

"Shut yo old crybaby ass up Dena, it ain't even like that, I just don't want for Carl to think that I've been fabricating how I'm living. I don't want this nigga to think that I got money based on how you live." Dena explained to her younger sister while nibbling on a strawberry from off of the tray of fresh fruit that had been placed around the theater.

At first, Dena felt the urge to sarcastically respond, but then again she looked at her big sister as if she was crazy.

"I tried to tell this dumb ass bitch that your money ain't her money. Girl, I asked her myself before we even came up in here, what in the fuck does your little sister's money have to do with you." Amina chimed in and said before Dawn could respond to what Dena had said to her in response.

All that Dena could do was throw up her hands, and bust out laughing at her older sister, with the rest of her crew. She couldn't understand why her income would lead to miscommunication between Dawn and her boo Carl.

"I think that it would be a great idea for you and your fiance to have your wedding here. And yo stupid ass better bring him over to my house prior too, I'm not playing with you Dawn." Dena swiftly said to her older sister while pointing at her with a carrot stick, somewhat lighting up the mood.

Although Dena had been younger than Dawn, Dena has always been the dominant of the two. Outside of their other siblings, Dawn and Dena's relationship was inappreciable. Dena may have stayed in the richer part of Piedmont, but please assure that Dawn wasn't too far away.

Dena noticed at the young age of five that her older sister would need her throughout life. Dena knew that her sister was hard-up for men, and she knew that her sister was gullible as well. Seeing with all of the stupid things that Dawn have done for her brothers while coming up as a child and throughout her adult life.

When Dena and Dawn turned eighteen, their parents decided on moving out of California. Unlike all of their other siblings, Dena and Dawn decided to stay in the golden state. Seeing that their parents had owned the house that they lived in, Dena and Dawn decided to take on the responsibilities of the home that their parents left behind. Leaving their parents clear and free of all debt.

Once Dena graduated from college, Dawn received low housing while Dena saved her money to later buy her small estate. Once Dena sealed the deal on her house, she decided on renting her parent's home out to someone on section eight.

Dena figured that this would be a way for her parents to make extra income, seeing that the house had been paid off in full. With the money that the government had been sending every month for rent, Dena made life easier for her parents by placing that money on their current accumulated bills.

Dena was the breadwinner of their entire family, and she made sure that her siblings along with her parents lived well as she did. Seeing that Dena hadn't had any kids, her obligation throughout life had been devoted to her family and friends.

One thing that Dena hadn't liked, was to look as if she'd been high siding on her siblings, and shaming her parents. With that being said, Dena always assured security towards her family first, and then her friends.

"Okay, so what movie we finna watch, or are we about to sit up here and listen to Dawn's dumb ass about embarrassing her man." Amina abruptly said while flopping onto the sofa and kicking her feet up on the atom.

Dena burst out into a peal of laughter from the comment that Amina just made towards Dawn. Seeing that Dena had enough of hearing about Dawn's excuse for never wanting to bring over her man. She'd been enlightened that Amina's rude outspoken ass switched up the mood.

"Look at Dena laughing at your simple ass, I know damn well that she's tired of hearing about that dumb ass shit too." Amina sarcastically said while filling around her waist searching for the remote control.

The four women sat on the huge sectional sofa fascinated with the movie that they'd finally agreed on watching. Seeing that the woman could never easily come to a mutual agreement, they would argue and bicker over just about any and everything that came along with making any choices or decisions.

That night the four women unknowingly drifted off on the sectional sofa. By the Time Taj awaken from her sleep, she realized that none of them left that night. Instead of Taj waking the rest of the girls up to leave, she decided on getting comfortable on the sofa, as she quickly drifted back off to sleep.

Ayseana left her home earlier than usual that morning, feeling alone and empty inside. Seeing that she isolated herself from her family and friends, she had no one to talk to whenever she felt like venting.

Ayseana had been feed up with her life, and she'd been disappointed with her so-called husband. It may have seemed like Ayseana had the perfect life on the outside, however, deep down inside, Ayseana had been dying.

Ayseana didn't have many friends or associates in Los Angeles seeing that she devoted all of her time to her husband and career.

Not only had Ayseana been embarrassed throughout the city of Los Angeles by her husband. But she'd also been humiliated, Ayseana didn't have anyone to console in, and she didn't have anyone that she could trust. Seeing that her husband introduced her to every last one of her new fake friends. Ayseana didn't have anyone to talk to without every single word that rolled off of her tongue getting back to her husband.

That morning when Ayseana pulled into the parking lot of her filming studio, she sat in her car for an hour. Ayseana had been confused about her marriage, and she'd been confused about the choice that she made to create her new self-image. Ayseana felt as if she sold her soul to the devil to satisfy her man. Ayseana felt within herself that she settled for the better of gratifying a man, and she'd felt as if she settled for less instead of the best.

"Humph, I wonder what in the fuck this nigga would do if I decided on packing up all of my shit and leaving." Ayseana questioned herself while stepping out of her Mercedes and headed towards the entrance of her dressing room.

That morning while filming, Ayseana based her entire segment on the misconduct of men and marriage. Seeing that so many women had been hurt and scorned, Ayseana had her entire studio audience and staff's undivided attention.

"We've all been hurt by a man, and we've all been simple for a man as well. No matter how hard we try to convince ourselves, as a woman that we deserve better, or even equal as a man, it will always run on dead ears. You know why because we'll always be considered naive by a man and only a woman. If you ever want to hurt a man's feelings, do something without him, and be sure to do it ten times better than he would!" Ayseana softly said to her large studio audience while silently thinking of her own personal problems with her husband.

After filming that afternoon, Ayseana went to her dressing room to grasp everything that she just said. Ayseana knew that her marriage was a front, and she'd known that she wasn't happy with the lifestyle that she lived.

"I need to start taking my own motherfucking advice, while I'm out here talking. Humph, that seemed to have always been one of my mother fucking problems, and here I am now making money off of this shit. Um, I don't know what to do with my life right now, I left the Bay because gossiping damn near made my friend lose her job." Ayseana reminded herself while rambling through the selection of alcohol that had been neatly placed on a bar-like shelf.

Just as Ayseana selected the bottle of Moet, she was quickly startled by the distraction of a light tap on her dressing room door.

"Yes." Ayseana softly yelled out, while pouring herself a glass of campaign, and looking towards the door.

"Mrs. Lewis, may I come in." Ayseana's assistant asked her from the other side of the door.

Once Ayseana noticed the voice on the other end of the door, she quickly placed her champagne down on the small bar frame to walk over and welcome him in.

"Come in, come in, yes, please do come in." Ayseana said to her assistant while eagerly flagging her hand for him to step

inside.

Ayseana's dressing room at the filming studio had been immaculate. It had been set up like a small studio apartment, seeing that she spent most of her time there filming. The producers always assured that Ayseana been comfortable as hell whenever filming at their studio. And for this reason, she was pampered with many luxuries and amenities.

"Well, spit it out. How may I help you?" Ayseana eagerly asked her assistant seeing that she noticed him looking around casing out her dressing room.

Seeing that Ayseana assistant was hand-picked by her husband, she learned early on that she couldn't trust him at all.

"Is it okay if we sit down for a moment Mrs. Lewis?" Ayseana assistant politely asked her, while politely taking a seat himself.

At this point, Ayseana hadn't known how to feel, and she suddenly started feeling strange and weird. Seeing that her assistant never seemed so serious ever before.

Before taking her assistant up on his offer, Ayseana

walked over to retrieve her glass of Moet while politely offering him a glass.

"No thank you, Mrs. Lewis." Her assistant said while flagging one of his fingers out at her with a no gesture.

Ayseana noticed that her assistant had been sitting stiff-backed with both of his legs held tightly together. She further noticed that whatever he wanted meant strict business for the both of them.

"Mrs. Lewis, I wanted to let you know that I have some good and bad news for you this afternoon. As you may know, your husband has been doing whatever it is that he may do. But he wanted for me to let you know that he'll be no longer managing you. And he also wanted for me to give you this." Ayseana assistant quietly said to her while handing her a small envelope.

Before Ayseana had the chance to open the neatly folded letter, she heard the sound of her dressing room door closing. Just as she looked up to notice that her assistant was leaving her with some sort of fabricated news about her husband.

Ayseana decided on sitting back down as she scanned through the letter that her assistant abruptly left her to privately read.

Just as Ayseana zoomed in and focused on the bold words on the front of the letter. She grew with a furious rage that she'd never shown before. The letter boldly read that her husband filed for a divorce. Ayseana was pissed off once she noticed that she'd been served a subpoena and had been reliable to pay spousal support.

"THIS DIRTY SON OF A BITCH!" Ayseana screamed out loud to the top of her lungs at no one in particular.

Ayseana grew so upset with herself that she quickly grabbed her purse and stormed out of her dressing room, loudly slamming the door close behind her.

Seeing that Ayseana's staff already been aware of the bad news, they made sure to stay been clear of the area that she was in.

Ayseana stormed out towards the parking lot raging mad seeing that she'd been robbed by her husband. Ayseana vision was blurry as she stomped to her car in an angry frustrated rage.

"I can't believe this selfish greedy, conniving, roguish mother fucker!" Ayseana *continued to yell out loud to herself while beating on her steering wheel with a face full of tears.*

Seeing that Ayseana left her studio in such a blatant rage late that afternoon. Ayseana hadn't come to realize that she was headed towards the grapevine.

Ayseana blacked out when she left her filming studio, and all she could think of was the comfort and support of her family and friends.

When Taj, Dena, Dawn, and Amina woke up the next morning, Taj couldn't help but mention Ayseana's name.

"Aye, y'all no who I've been thinking about lately." Taj asked the group of girls while eating a heaping scope of her maple and brown sugar oatmeal that morning.

"Who, that nigga that you played out of a trip to France, and left in his feelings last week." Amina playfully interrupted her and said, while laughing out loud with Dena and Dawn joining in.

"No bitch! I'm serious ass fuck right now, and you wanna keep playing. I'm talking about Ayseana." Taj questioned her

three best friends while looking directly at them.

Amina, rolled her eyes at the thought of Ayseana name, seeing that she ran off on all four of them during their toughest times.

"I could give two fat fucks about the lame-ass bitch." Amina boldly said while popping her neck towards Taj to assure that her feelings and reactions towards their other so-called best friend were understood.

"Well, I don't feel that way Amina, I mean she was and still is considered our best friend and sister. Right?" Dena questioned her group of friends despite how Amina may have felt.

Dawn kept quiet about the whole situation seeing that she felt the same way as Amina. Dawn on the other hand also refused on going against her younger sister, seeing that she only been concerned about her and Carl's upcoming wedding.

"Well, despite what Amina's old evil ass has to say, I still miss her, and it's been years since we've last seen her. Taj emphasized to her friends while taking another scope of her now loop warm oatmeal.

The woman sat around and discussed Ayseana for a few more hours, before getting dressed to head their separate ways later that morning.

Before everyone left Dena's home that day, they agreed that they'd later look into looking for Ayseana. With Dena being a forensic pathologist, and with Taj now being the DA, they had no problem with locating their best friend fast.

Ayseana snapped out her trance just as she drove down highway ninety-nine through Chowchilla.

"Where in the hell am I going? And what in the fuck do I think I'm doing." Ayseana asked herself while pulling off of the highway and into a service station.

Ayseana pulled into a random gas station as if she was getting gas, only to debate with herself, her final destination. Although Ayseana abandoned her family and friends over the years, Ayseana knew deep down inside that she was always come back home.

"I don't know what in the hell I'm thinking." Ayseana questioned herself while letting out a huge sigh to revive her of the anxiety and stress that she heavily carried.

BLACK BARBIE

"Imma get a room, yea that's what I'll do. I'll get a room first, then I'll continue my drive to the Bay first thing tomorrow morning. If I get indecisive or distracted, I'll just pull over again and get myself another room until I feel comfortable." Ayseana told herself, as she came to an agreeance with assuring herself on what she'd do next.

Seeing that it had been late into the night, Ayseana was exhausted as she sat in the middle of nowhere mesmerized. Ayseana couldn't believe what she'd been going through, and she couldn't believe that she was headed back home to the Bay Area. Ayseana pulled out her cellphone, to look up her navigation and locate a decent hotel nearby.

After checking into the room, and finally being able to lay down and rest. Ayseana drifted off into a swift sleep that left her restless and stressed. The next morning when Ayseana woke up from her well-needed rest. She felt alive, revived, and refreshed although she went to bed tense and depressed.

Despite everything that went on with Ayseana before that day. Ayseana was ready to finish her journey back home to her family and friends despite her five-year or so disappearance.

Reality started to settle in once Ayseana crossed the Altima Pass and had been less than thirty minutes outside of Oakland. Ayseana palms started to sweat as her nerves began to rattle, Ayseana started to get nervous and second guess herself despite how she previously felt.

"You no what Ayseana, you got this." Ayseana told herself with a little prep talk as she took the ninety-eighth Avenue exit.

Seeing that Taj and Ayseana had grown up together, she felt that it would be best for her to reach out to Taj first.

Soon as Ayseana pulled her Mercedes in front of Taj's house, the memories started flowing in. Everything that crossed Ayseana mind brought a huge smile upon her face that she hadn't felt in years.

"Fuck this shit! I miss my mother fucking friends." Ayseana boldly told herself as she hopped out of her car headed towards Taj's front door.

Ding dong ding dong, ding dong, ding dong, was the outrageous sound of Ayseana drastically pressing on Taj's doorbell.

Taj on the other hand had been sitting in the living room of her home, going over a few court cases when she noticed her doorbell chiming out of control at the other end.

At first, Taj hadn't paid the erratic ringing of her doorbell any attention, seeing that she hadn't been expecting anyone to stop by and visit. Taj carried on with her work reminiscing with herself the way that Ayseana always ranged her doorbell similar to the way that it was being ranged that moment. Taj had been deep in her work and somewhat daydreaming about her and Ayseana when she came to realize that the doorbell ringing was a reality.

Taj calmly removed her paperwork from the center of her lap, as she got up to see who had been ringing her doorbell from the other end.

Instead of Taj asking who was on the other side of the door before opening it. Taj swung the door wide open to greet her long-time best friend.

"Oh my God Ayseana, is it really you, wherein the hell have you been!" Taj excitedly and eagerly asked her while fanning her face from any unwanted tears.

That moment when Taj greeted Ayseana at her front door, everything went into a tailspin. Ayseana didn't have a chance to say a word, as Taj shuffled her into the house closing the door shut behind them.

Taj had so much that she wanted to share with Ayseana until she hadn't known where to begin. Taj didn't know if she wanted to share the good news of Dawn's wedding or keep their conversation basic.

The only thing that Taj had known for certain, was that she wanted to apologize to Ayseana for throwing her out of her house the way that she did a few years back.

Taj wanted to clear the guilt on her back for enticing Ayseana to run off and disappear for as long as she did. Taj wanted to further let Ayseana know that she deeply missed her sister and best friend.

"I don't know where to start Seana, I should not have blown upon you the way that I did." Taj explained to Ayseana while now holding both of her hands.

Ayseana looked at Taj with a broken heart seeing that she wished that she too would not of left Taj's house the way that she did.

"You don't have to apologize to me Taj, you didn't do anything wrong. If you've done something wrong to me Taj, I wouldn't be sitting here with you now." Ayseana explained to Taj while freeing one of her hands to wipe away Taj's tears.

Once Taj and Ayseana confided in each other by talking over what happened in the past. Taj excitedly explained to Ayseana that they've all assumed that she deliberately went missing. Taj further informed Ayseana that it hadn't been until recently when they all found out that she moved to LA.

Ayseana and Taj talked for hours that afternoon filling each other in on the good and bad things that'd been going on in their lives. By the time the girls finished reuniting, they decided on pulling up on Dena, Dawn, and Amina later that night.

"You know what." Taj thought out loud.

"I'm not going to tell them that you're here, I'm going to arrange for dinner reservations and have you pop up. You know, I want for you to surprise them, and see the reactions on their face the same way that you've done with me. Besides, we have a lot to catch up on, we're sisters first, and of course best friends." Taj

eagerly reminded Ayseana with a huge smile across her face,
doing her best to make Ayseana feel wanted.

Relentless

Once the girls merged back together, Dawn and Amina both had mixed feelings for Ayseana and her sudden abrupt return. Dawn and Amina weren't as welcoming as Taj and Dena, seeing that they could tell Ayseana was holding something back from them.

After dinner that night, Ayseana checked into her hotel room, as Dena, Taj, Amina, and Dawn went separate ways. Once Amina and dawn made it home that night, they called each other up on their cellphones to discuss what they witnessed first hand.

"Can you believe that this weird-ass bitch just popped back up like nothing ever happened." Amina explained to Dawn over the phone while lying across her king-size bed.

Dawn and Amina went back and forth with each other over the phone for twenty minutes discussing Ayseana instead of what happened overall during dinner that night.

Dawn and Amina were so wrapped up in their conversation as to why Ayseana suddenly came back into town.

Until they both gave themselves a headache before hanging up their cellphones that night.

The next few weeks while Ayseana was in town Dena and Taj had been busy at work leaving Dawn and Amina with extra time on their hands. Instead of Amina and Dawn preparing for Dawn's wedding like they should've been doing or showing Ayseana a good time. Dawn and Amina did the exact opposite.

Without Taj or Dena to point Dawn and Amina in the right direction, Dawn and Amina always seemed to get easily distracted. Whenever the two women became distracted, it never seemed to turn out good.

For some odd reason, Dawn and Amina hatched a plan to do an investigation on their long-time lost and found a best friend.

"I wanna no why this bitch just up and left LA." Amina *explained to Dawn while googling Ayseana information.*

Amina felt as if Ayseana had been leaving a lot of information out about her personal life. And Amina felt that Ayseana was holding back something, seeing that she'd been gone for the last five years.

"I mean, I do feel what you're saying and all." Dawn hesitantly said to Amina while leaning over the marble countertop of her kitchen to get a glance at what Amina was reading on her laptop.

Meanwhile, Dawn tried her best to focus back on her wedding arrangements by assuring Amina that everything had previously been prepared. Seeing that Dawn tried her best not to get twisted up into Amina's madness, Dawn found any excuse for her and Amina to continue focusing on her wedding.

"Owe bitch, you see what the fuck I'm talking about, this bullshit right here." Amina excitedly yelled out to Dawn while turning towards her to show her exactly what she just found on her laptop.

Seeing that Amina had been persistent in her quest on digging up any information that she could on Ayseana. Dawn grown tempted into finding out about Ayseana as well, seeing that Amina insisted on pressuring her to get in Ayseana's business.

"See bitch, I told you that this bitch still ain't shit. I mean, why she gotta lie to us though? Why she out here acting like we

ain't her real best friends?" Amina questioned Dawn while *allowing her to scroll through her laptop to see for herself what she found.*

Dawn remained quiet while she viewed the details of Ayseana's lifestyle over the past five years. Amina sat quietly on the side of Dawn, watching her scroll down the website on her laptop shocked and disgruntled. Far as Amina had been concerned, Ayseana had been fake with all four of them from the moment they meet.

"Wait a minute Amina, let's not be so quick to judge. Have you taken out the time to read what you've actually seen?" Dawn questioned her while holding Amina's laptop to her face, pointing at the screen indicating what she'd been reading.

Dawn explained to Amina that it seemed as if Ayseana had been in an abusive relationship or situation. Dawn further went on to tell Amina that it seemed to her as if Ayseana came to them in her time of need.

"Yea I hear what you saying and all, and I understand all of that your reading. But the bottom line is that this bitch burnt rubber on us in our time of need! So please explain to me why in

the hell she came back in need of our friendship. I could literally give two flat fucks about what she's going through. Obviously, she's been going through it for five years! Am I right or wrong, that fake ass bitch can keep running to whomever she's been going to for the last five years!" Amina sarcastically yelled out at Dawn while walking over towards Dena's small minibar to pour herself a drink.

"Damn bitch, it seems as if Ayseana got you heated, huh sis." Dawn playfully asked Amina while turning her attention back to her wedding instead of attending to Amina and Ayseana's bullshit.

"We're supposed to be making last-minute wedding arrangements right now. Meanwhile, you out here worried about some other shit that's beyond you and me. Can we please focus back on what we can control!" Dawn exaggerated to Amina while turning around to face her as she proudly stood at the minibar.

Amina rolled her eyes at Dawn as she proudly poured herself another shot of Hennessy.

"Well, like it or not, I'm going to say something about it at lady's night next week." Amina reminded Dawn while swishing

around her shoot of Hennessy and swallowing it with one gulp.

The next weekend at lady's night, things hadn't gone as Amina would've liked. Seeing that Ayseana hadn't been able to attend due to filming.

With Amina having a devious plan to boldly burst Ayseana out in front of all of their friends. Amina had been so pissed off with Ayseana's absence until she decided on telling all of her business to Taj and Dena without her being there to speak up on her own behalf.

"Whelp, I figured that she wouldn't be here this weekend anyway, seeing that Dawn and I have done a little digging into her disappearance." Amina swiftly explained to her group of friends while placing emphases on what she'd been saying all while looking directly at Taj.

"First off, I don't have shit to do with this, you a got damn lie about whatever it is that you got to say! Specifically, if the bullshit got my name all up in it, don't come up in here lying to them talking about some me and Dawn. Bullshit! Yo ass was the one who sat up there and googled that girl's business!" Dawn boldly interrupted Amina and swiftly said while defending herself

from what might happen.

Seeing that Dawn refused on being entwined with Amina's bullshit. Dawn and Amina went back and forth with each other arguing about Ayseana until Dena and Taj had been confused.

Taj and Dena had been so confused about what had been going on until they both tried their best to make sense of the situation.

"Hold up now, y'all keep yapping and going back and forth with each other while this whole conversation makes absolutely no sense for either Dena or myself!" Taj yelled out to both Dawn and Amina while abruptly interrupting their private engagement.

Amina, Taj, and Dena had all been sitting on Dawn's back porch trying their best to enjoy the moon that was settling in. Before Dawn and Amina decided to get into their private altercation without inviting Taj and Dena.

After sitting in silence for five minutes, Amina and Dawn swiftly looked at each other sarcastically before responding to Taj.

Seeing that Amina had decided to investigate Ayseana's personal business. Dawn decided on giving Amina the look of destruction, as she sat up in her lounge chair and arrogantly decided to speak.

"Well bitch, gone and tell them what you found out! I mean, it ain't like you haven't been dying to tell them anyway." Dawn sarcastically snapped at Amina and said while peeking over her designer replica frames in Amina's direction and comfortably lying back in her lounge chair.

Amina looked at Dawn as if she lost her ever-lasting mind seeing that Amina hadn't been ready to spill all of her tea.

Seeing that Dawn didn't want to be implicated with Amina's bullshit. Dawn threw Amina under the bus and forced her to share what she dug up on Ayseana with Taj and Dena.

With Amina having a little more investigating to do, she hadn't been quite ready to gossip without Ayseana's presence. Amina needed Ayseana there to fill them in with all of the blanks and she needs for Ayseana to come out with the truth.

"Bitch, I thought that we were better than that!" Amina sarcastically snapped at Dawn while knocking Dawn's sun hat

from off top of her head.

Dawn jumped up from out of her lounge chair as if she'd seen a ghost. She tried her best to catch her sunhat from falling out of the air and onto the ground. Taj and Dena both turned to look at Dawn and Amina as if they'd lost their everlasting minds.

"What in the hell is going on here with you two?" Dena surprisingly asked them with no hesitation.

Dena and Taj continued to look at each other with suspense upon their faces as they tried their best to figure out what in the hell Dawn and Amina were talking about.

"Aright bitch damn, you minus well go on ahead and fill my sister and Taj in. And bitch the next time you touch my Dior sunhat, you better recall. I ain't no killer but don't push me." Dawn jokingly yelled out to Amina while sticking out her tong and throwing up the middle finger.

Meanwhile, Dena and Taj had been eager to hear what they've found out about Ayseana. Hell, at this point, Dena and Taj were excited to hear about anyone that they might have known or known of.

The main thing that Dena and Taj wanted to get to the bottom of, was what in the hell had Dawn and Amina been bickering about Ayseana.

"Can you two bitches please stop playing around, and spit that shit out. Got damn, you bitches out here playing with my anticipation." Taj sarcastically said while now leaning on the edge of her lawn chair at full attention.

Seeing that the spotlight had now been sat on Amina, who'd been standing front and center ready to entertain.

Not only was Amina eager to share with Taj and Dena what she'd dug up on Ayseana, but she was excited, eager ready, and willing to spill the beans.

Amina placed herself in front of Taj, Dena, and Dawn as if she'd been standing center stage. Amina stood proudly in front of all three of her homegirls ready to gossip. She stood as if she'd been standing on stage at the Paramount Theater in Oakland, California ready to entertain a large crowd.

"First off, I wanna start by asking Taj, what did Ayseana tell you when she first came to you. You know what I mean, what did she say when she first popped back up into town. I know she

came to you first, I found out that she hadn't stopped by her mom's house until she was getting ready to head back towards Los Angeles." Amina softly questioned Taj while stretching her arms straight out in front of her as if she was holding a lecture and pointing directly at Taj.

Taj looked at Amina clueless, seeing that she had the slightest idea of what Amina was talking about or trying to get at. Before Taj could answer Amina's questions, Amina started right back up from her previous conversation all while ignoring Taj's delayed response.

"Okay cool, no worries! I understand that you're not able to answer that question right away." Amina sarcastically told Taj before getting deep off into her conversation.

Once Amina cleared the air with what she found out about Ayseana earlier that week. Everyone suddenly picked up their cellphones and began to chime in with various opinions.

"You know what, now that you've mentioned it, she never once mentioned anything about her personal life. She never said anything outside of her TV career for the last five years. Maybe we aren't as tight as we think." Taj questioned herself out loud to no

one in particular while standing with both of her arms folded on top of her breast in deep thought.

"Five years can do a lot to a person. I mean I've heard of people changing overnight, howsoever I could only imagine the changes that five years could suddenly bring. But if she consider us as her sisters and best friends, why would she lie to us. And why would she decide to show up open heartily with no consideration after five years." Dena presumptuously replied to Taj and said while looking everyone directly in the face as she spoke with emphasis and deep concern.

Amina, Dawn, and Taj all looked at Deana surprisingly, seeing that she never looked at the negative in any situation. With Dena bringing more attention to Ayseana's reappearance, the women made it their point to get deep into Ayseana's business.

Ayseana had been back at home in the Hollywood Hills of Los Angeles with more bad news. Not only had she lost her husband and had been suddenly going through an unwanted divorce. But Ayseana suddenly received word that her show had also been canceled.

Seeing that Ayseana's husband had been her manager,

and tended to all of her finances along with her contracts. Ayseana turned out to be an even bigger fool without knowing about it.

Ayseana's husband found her at a desperate time and mysteriously swept her from off of her feet. She'd been eager and selfish to wholeheartedly place all of her trust into one mysterious man that she later called her husband.

Ayseana sat on a bar stole of what use to be her marble countertop with a fifth of Hennessy and a face full of tears. She reflected on the past five years of her life with every harsh bitter sip.

Ayseana reminisced on the way her soon-to-be ex-husband approached her in the lobby at motel six when they first meet. She reminded herself about the way he persuaded her into taking on her new fame and career.

Ayseana stood next to her kitchen counter staring at the empty bottle that was once a fifth of Hennessy confused. She stood there in a daze, plotting on various ways of getting revenge with her husband.

"I can't do this by myself." Ayseana whined out loud while

forming soft tears in the corner of her eyes.

"I need my friends." Ayseana continued to carry on with herself while now sobbing uncontrollably.

At first, Ayseana decided on calling up Taj and filling her in on everything that she'd been going through. But, then again, her pride advised her not to.

Ayseana suddenly reminded herself that she'd always been a failure to her family and friends. She reminded herself that the last thing she needed was questions and judgment about her choices and decisions.

Ayseana was confused, with no one to confide in and she refused on starting her life over from rock bottom with absolutely nothing.

"Hell no, that's the last thing that I'll ever do again! When I left that big raggedy mother fucking city I didn't have shit, and I'll be damn if I return with nothing!" Ayseana murmured to herself while suddenly stopping her flow of random tears.

Ayseana stood straight up from her slumber over the kitchen counter, as she suddenly jumped up and sprinted down the long hallway. Ayseana bolted up the spiral stairs as she suddenly picked up a random idea.

Ayseana stood in the doorway of her master bedroom casually looking around as if she was in observance of something in particular.

"I know that this mother fucker better be still in my safe!" Ayseana yelled out to herself as she made her way towards her bedroom closet.

Once Ayseana walked inside of her closet, she set her eyes towards the back far left corner. She ignored the elaborate mink coats and fur vest that were neatly hung throughout with an abundance of designer brands amongst a few other things.

Ayseana's focus was simultaneously on what she abruptly wanted, she coincidentally had tunnel vision.

Ayseana crouched down in the back of her closet to locate her safe. Without any hesitation or second-guessing, Ayseana quickly entered the combination into her safe yanking the door open.

Ayseana yanked the door open so hard until she fell flat

on her back. Ayseana was in a rage, and she quickly bounced herself right back up to retrieve her Glock forty-five fully loaded handgun. Exactly what she'd swiftly decided on running up to her bedroom and probing through her safe for.

Ayseana leaned her back up against the wall of her closet while looking down the barrel of her gun. She seemed groggy and bewildered from the fifth of Hennessy that she drunken earlier that evening. She swiftly flashed through bits and pieces of her life with absolutely no emotion or thought to console herself.

Taj, Dawn, Amina, and Dena had all woke up that Sunday morning as usual when having lady's night at Dena's. That night, the girls had been quiet while enjoying a light brunch and dabbling at the table with different things amongst each other and themselves.

Taj had been sitting at the left of the table going through the emails in her phone while sipping on a small cup of espresso and indulging in a piece of dry toast.

Dena on the other hand had been sitting at the head of the table, thumbing through her old social media pages seeing what she could find out about Ayseana. She never once seemed to have tended to her small bowl of fruit that sat directly in front of her on the table.

Dawn and Amina sat next to each other at the table doing the same as Dena had been. The only difference with them was that they enjoyed their eggs and bacon as they scrolled through their phones digging for anything interesting.

The women sat at brunch that morning in total silence for forty-five minutes before the maid walked in and broke their concentration and silence.

"Are you ladies finished, may I clean up your dishes my dear." An older black woman had questioned Dena while reaching out for her bowl of fruit that she hadn't touched.

"Oh yes ma'am, you're fine, we're all finished here." Dena kindly replied to her house servant while softly patting her on the shoulders.

Taj, Amina, and Dawn had taken heed to Dena's message towards her house servant and immediately removed themselves from the table.

Once the ladies gathered in the foyer and briefly spoke for a few moments, the trio immediately left Dena's house right after brunch late that afternoon.

Taj, Amina, and Dawn rode home in complete silence and deep thought about their use to be best friend and sister Ayseana.

Seeing that Amina stayed in San Francisco, Dawn and Taj decided on indulging in a little conversation of their own on their way back across the bridge.

"How do you fill Taj, I mean you haven't said much since you found out. I mean hell, you haven't said anything at all." Dawn had outspokenly said while turning down the volume to the radio assuring that Taj had been able to hear what she asked.

Taj had taken a deep sigh, while slightly taking her eyes from off of the road to look sympathetically in Dawn's face.

"I mean, to tell you the truth Dawn, I don't know how to feel. I can for sure tell you that it fucked me up. I mean, on one hand, it made me think about what Dena had said, you no the five-year thing. Like we ain't hear shit from Ayseana when she was doing good, and suddenly she popped up when she's going

through a divorce. Mind you, Dawn, this dumb ass bitch don't know that we know she's going through a divorce." Taj replied to Dawn while aggressively smacking her lips and focusing on the road ahead of her.

"Well, has she tried reaching back out to you since she left back to LA?" Dawn asked her while readjusting herself in the front seat.

"Nah, she hasn't called me or Dena, and we both gave that sneaky bitch our phone numbers. Me and Dena both asked this bitch to let us know when she safely landed back in town." Taj had further gone on to say in response to Dawn's question.

Taj and Dawn went on about Ayseana's conniving ways for the rest of their ride. By the time Taj dropped Dawn off at home, she found herself fighting with her conscious about reaching out to Ayseana.

"I really should call this bitch and let her know about herself." Taj said to no one in particular as she walked through her front door entryway.

Taj had thrown her bags down of the marble floor directly where she stood, as she walked over towards her living room couch to toss her purse on the sofa. She casually kicked off her shoes while strolling towards the kitchen to open up her refrigerator and grab herself a soda. While standing at the fridge with the door wide open, Taj downed her orange Fanta soft drink in damn near one sip.

"Woo, I needed that, after all of this weekend tea." Taj murmured to herself while walking towards her living room to enjoy a random show on TV.

Dawn had been at home with her husband, preparing the finishing touches for her wedding all while filling her husband in on all of their girl talk and tea.

"Baby I'm just glad that nobody told her about the wedding. I'm glad that we decided on not saying anything." Dawn explained to her husband all while smiling and staring directly at in his face.

Carl had been sitting on the opposite end of the couch enjoying a college football game as he half hardily listened to what Dawn had been saying. If Carl hadn't known about anything else, he knew how to satisfy Dawn, and he knew how to balance out his time for himself.

Seeing that Dawn spent most of her Saturdays with her friends, and Carl spent his Saturdays mentoring kids. Sundays had always been set aside as a time for just them.

Dawn hadn't cared if her man had been enjoying the game while listening to her gossip and complain. The only thing that Dawn cared about and appreciated, was that she was at home stress-free with her soon-to-be husband.

Unlike Ayseana's marriage, Dawn and Carl had taken their time with each other. They both wanted one another, and they both wanted their relationship to work.

Dawn and Carl may not have had the money that Ayseana and her husband had. However, Carl and Dawn had the genuine loving connection that Ayseana fabricated to her so-called sisters and best friends.

Ayseana had damn near lost her mind off of that fifth of Hennessy that she swiftly drunk as if it was a cold Pepsi earlier that day. Ayseana sat alone in her dimmed closet for more than an hour looking down the barrel of her gun drunk and dizzy.

"My life ain't shit, I wonder how everyone would fill if I suddenly took my life. I wonder how my bitch ass husband would

feel. I wonder if he'd fill some type of remorse for building me up and then tearing me down!" Ayseana questioned herself with a face full of tears.

"I fucking hate it here!" Ayseana screamed out to the top of her lungs before sticking the barrel of her forty-five inside her mouth aimed at the back of her throat.

"Do it bitch, do it now bitch, don't be no punk ass bitch. Makes these mother fuckers out here feel yo pain sis." Ayseana told herself with the barrel of her gun still shoved in her mouth.

Ayseana sat in her closet at full attention in a deep cold sweat. She constantly opened and closed her eyes as she deeply contemplated on pulling the trigger. She swiftly rocked her body back and forth without thinking or second-guessing as she quickly pulled the trigger.

A loud boom went out with a spark of fire as Ayseana head slammed into the back of her closet wall with her brain splattered into a million bits and pieces. Her body jerked and shock as her nervous system suddenly reacted to the gun's blast and explosion.

Ayseana had cheated herself out of life due to per-

pressure and unwanted exposure. She had hidden the true meaning of herself from all of her family and friends. She wanted for her husband to love her, and she wanted for her husband to walk in on what she had done to herself. When in reality, the housekeeper had been the one to stumble upon her mangled and demised body that started to root away in her walk-in closet.

It had been almost three months since anyone had heard from Ayseana. Her housekeeper had decided on letting herself in at the request of Ayseana ex-husband.

The housekeeper went about her normal routine before stumbling upon Ayseana body despite the foul odor throughout the house. Once the maid finally walked upstairs to the master bedroom the foul order that she'd been smelling throughout the house, had quickly hit her nose.

"Oh no, no, me no like the way that stank smell, me no exactly what that smell is." The housekeeper said to herself with a broken accent while swiftly walking down the stairs.

The housekeeper assumed that Ayseana's husband had either killed her or had her killed, seeing that he was the only one that she was able to get in contact with.

The housekeeper went into a sudden panic, seeing that she'd been all too familiar with stumbling upon dead bodies throughout various homes in the Hollywood hills.

Instead of the housekeeper calling the police to Ayseana home like she should have done, she panicked and returned home to her husband and family.

Seeing that Ayseana housekeeper had been an illegal citizen, she'd been terrified about notifying the police.

The last time Ayseana's housekeeper notified the police about another homicide at a different home she'd been caring for. The LA police treated her like a suspect instead of a witness and threatened to deport her and her family if she didn't corporate and testify for them.

Ayseana's housekeeper debated with her family for six weeks after noticing the foul smell of death in Ayseana home. After confiding with her husband, Ayseana's housekeeper finally decided on calling LAPD and leaving an anonymous tip on what she thinks may have happened.

"Ey, yes, is dis da policia? Ey, I have a tep about a dead person." The housekeeper hesitantly said over the phone in broken English.

The housekeeper quickly spoke with the police receptionist over a payphone in a neighboring city outside of where she lived.

Although the housekeeper agreed about reporting the incident with her family. Ayseana's housekeeper had known from past experience better than to let the police know exactly who she was.

After the housekeeper gave LAPD grave detail on what she assumed may have happened, she abruptly disconnected the payphone. Unbeknownst to the housekeeper, she was in fact the first person that the detectives would later question.

Dawn and her new husband Carl recently enjoyed their wedding, and they'd just came back from enjoying their honeymoon. Only to later share with her friends and family that she and Carl would be expecting their first child together soon.

Amina continued hustling in the city while living out the elaborate lifestyle of the fast life. After being at Dawn's wedding, she never mentioned much more about Ayseana, nor had she dug up any further information.

Taj and Dena continued to bury themselves with work, seeing that cases had been coming by the truckloads.

After Dawn's wedding, Taj and Dena barely had time to enjoy the reception. With Dawn having to base the schedule of her wedding around Taj and Dena's work schedule. Dena and Taj both unanimously agreed upon paying for everything at the wedding while arranging for it to be exactly how Dawn wanted.

Seeing that Dawn couldn't resist the offer of an elaborate free wedding, she couldn't complain about the needed accommodations. With Amina further offering to purchase her dress, all Dawn needed to do was find the perfect man to fall in love with.

All four of the woman now focused on themselves and doing their own thing throughout life. Dawn, Amina, Dena, and Taj rarely had time for each other, let alone time for themselves.

Seeing that Ayseana always decided on randomly disappearing, the woman hadn't noticed that she was nonexistent.

Not only had it been almost five months since the LAPD found Ayseana decomposed body. But it had also been the last time since Ayseana visited with Dena, Taj, Amina, and Dawn.

With Ayseana only having her husband listed on all of her emergency contact and contact records, the police only notified him after questioning.

Ayseana husband was so spiteful and vindictive of her new lifestyle and career. Until he dismissed her death in passing, he hadn't reached out to her mother, nor had he considered reaching out to her fans or friends. Ayseana husband had been so disrespectful of her death until he kept her suicide hidden from the press. No one had a clue on what happened to Ayseana, nor were they aware that she was no longer in existence.

It had taken for a local magazine to report the secret suicide as a headline on their front page cover a year later.

Amina had been hanging out in the beautiful city of San Francisco, doing what she did best on pill hill. She walked into one of the local stores that she frequent to grab herself something cold to drink, seeing that it been scorching hot outside that summer day.

For no reason in particular Amina decided on staying inside of the store a little longer so she could enjoy the cool breeze from the store's air conditioning.

Seeing that Amina didn't want the owner of the store to kick her out for loitering, she decided on drinking her ice-cold soda in front of the magazine stand.

Amina scanned the various selection of magazines as she casually sipped on her soda reading and scanning various headlines. Just as Amina placed the plastic soda bottle to the bottom of her lip for another sip, one magazine astonishingly attracted her attention.

Amina leaned over to read the details in the headline of the magazine, as she'd been shocked by what she'd seen. Amina focused on the magazine article as she went over Ayseana's name fifty times in her head to assure what she was reading.

At first, Amina seemed confused about what she'd been reading, she was shocked and dismayed. Amina wanted to assure herself that she'd been reading and seeing what she think she just read.

"Hey, are you going to buy something, or just stand there

and look stupid?" The store clerk yelled out from behind the front counter startling Amina from her deep gaze and daydream.

Amina jumped up as if she'd seen a ghost, once she comes to realize that the store owner had been yelling to get her attention.

Amina quickly placed the cap on her soda and set it to the side, as she picked up the entire stack of magazines advertising Ayseana death.

"Hey you, don't forget to pay for the soda that you've already opened!" The store clerk reminded her while pointing for her to go back over to the magazine rack and retrieve her beverage.

Amina quickly ran back over to the rack doing exactly what the store clerk asked of her. Her mind had gone blank and her feet had been in motion as she couldn't believe what she had in her hands.

"Wow, I see that you've bought us out, yea, this is a really popular magazine. You should read the first article, I swear that her husband is the one responsible for her death." The store clerk rambled on and said while bagging up Amina's things.

After leaving out of the store that evening, Amina rushed to her car to head across the bridge towards Oakland.

"Hay Dawn, it's an emergency, I need for you to contact Taj and tell her to meet us at Dena's house. I need you to let Dena know that it's urgent. Dawn let her know that we all need to meet up at her spot asap, as in right now." Amina yelled out through the phone with a face full of tears before hanging up in Dawn's face.

Dawn had been home alone that evening, she'd been startled by Amina's phone call. The tone in Amina's voice had let Dawn know that whatever it was, must have been serious.

Dawn quickly ran around her house gathering up her things as she patiently waited for Taj to pick her up.

"Oh my god Dawn what in the hell is going on, my fucking heart is racing. What did Amina say that she wanted, did she tell you why in the hell she was screaming." Taj questioned Dawn soon as she got inside of the car.

"I don't no Taj, all I know is that she sounded hysterical and serious about whatever it is. Oh my god I can't take this shit, I'm five months pregnant, and this bitch got me out her stressing."

Dawn reminded Taj while spreading her leg to comfortably rest her belly as she softly rubbed on it.

"Well don't stress the baby over it, whatever it is, it'll be okay, and it'll all be over soon." Taj assured Dawn while freeing her hand from the steering wheel to tap on her belly.

Although Dawn hadn't mentioned it to Taj, her stomach tightened up with bad cramps ever since Amina called her with shocking news.

"I don't know why in the fuck she called you first with this bullshit anyways, that bitch no your pregnant. Amina no mother fucking well that we can't have you out here stressing and shit. OM fucking G, Amina, Amina, Amina, this shit better be important! And this here bullshit better be worth the six o'clock news." Taj playfully said to Dawn trying her best to lighten up the mood.

Dawn glanced over at Taj with a half-hearted smile as she continued to quietly suffer from pains in her belly from her unborn baby.

"Are you okay over there? Because we can go to the hospital first, and wait to hear Amina's gossip and news later!"

Taj reminded Dawn while noticing that Dawn wasn't herself, all while noticing that she'd been uncomfortable in the passenger seat.

Dawn looked at Taj with a sarcastic stare, as she smacked her lips at what Taj said.

"Now girl you know that I want this scope, whatever it is, the shit has to be serious. Shit you the DA, you know damn well that these are her busiest hours." Dawn looked over at Taj and grunted and said.

Just as Taj and Dawn had been pulling up to Dena's front gate, they could see that Amina had just arrived ahead of them.

"Whelp, this must be important, the gangs all here, and right on time. She must have called you after she was already on the freeway." Taj had asked Dawn while helping her out of the SUV.

Dena had been on the front porch eager to greet everyone as they quickly walked in. Seeing that Amina hadn't given any information on the urgent meeting, everyone had been in a panic.

Amina swiftly walked past Dena, leading the way towards her formal dining room table with a plastic shopping bag held tight in her hands.

Taj, Dawn, and Dena looked at each other confused seeing that Amina hadn't said anything until they all sat down at the table.

"Okay listen." Amina said to the girls with a face full of tears still holding tight to the magazines that were wrapped tight in her arms.

"Amina what's going on." Dawn scarcely asked her with a look of fear and terror in her eyes.

"Dawn calm down please." Taj quickly requested of her once she noticed her rubbing her stomach from the tight pain that she'd been feeling from her baby.

Dena continued to sit in silence, as her mind rambled in a state of shock.

"Amina, please control yourself for god's sake, you're scaring my sister and she's pregnant!" Dena yelled out from frustration and fear.

Without another word being said, Amina proceeded to control her tears and genitally pass out the magazines that she bought at the corner store in the city earlier that day.

At first, the girls looked at Amina as if she'd lost her mind seeing that they still hadn't understood the point that she'd been desperately trying to make.

"Read the headlines, and then open it up." Amina ordered her friends while whipping off a face full of snot and tears.

"Oh my god!" Taj yelled out while scanning through the first few paragraphs of the article dedicated to Ayseana.

Dawn looked over at Taj with what seemed to be her eyes bulging out of her head once she comes to realize what she'd been reading. Her heart suddenly began to race, as her body started to shake and panic. The pains in her belly began to get tighter around the grip of her skin as she swiftly fell out of her chair from pain, frustration, and fear.

"OH MY GOD DAWN!" Amina yelled out as she dropped the remainder of the magazines that she'd been holding in her hands onto the floor.

Although Taj and Dena had been sitting closer to Dawn than Amina had been. Dena hadn't seemed to notice what happened to Dawn seeing that it happened so vastly.

"Somebody call the got damn ambulance!" Taj yelled out as she quickly ran to the kitchen to get Dawn a glass of water.

Dena damn near lost her mind in a desperate panic once she finally comes to realization. Seeing that Dena took things lightly she went into a desperate panic once she noticed Dawn's reaction.

With Dena now watching her older sister lie flat on her back in the middle of her dining room floor lifeless, Deana damn near fainted.

"Dena!" Taj yelled out once she noticed that Dena had been standing in the same place without ever picking up the phone to call for help.

Everything quickly went into cayuse, confusion, fear, worry, and sudden stress with an abundance of frustration and fear. The three women stood in the middle of the dining room dumbfounded as if they hadn't had the slightest clue on what to do.

"Okay, um here Amina, try to get this glass of water down Dawn's throat while I call nine-one-one." Taj shakingly said damn near spilling the glass of water all over Amina as she nervelessly passed it to her.

Taj sat Dena back down in the chair at the head of the table as she fumbled through her purse for her cellular phone. After speaking with the nine-one-one operator for less than three minutes, help was on the way.

By now, Dena's house staff caught on to what was going on and had been doing their best to offer Dawn assistance until the paramedics arrived.

Dena's eyes had been swollen from the sudden stress of tears, as she pounded on her marble table screaming out for the lord to comfort her fears.

"Lord Jesus father God why me, what have I done for you to bring me so much sudden grief and fear." Dena yelled out to no one in particular as she looked up at the ceiling of her home screaming and crying contentiously calling onto the Lord for help.

Taj leaned on the kitchen counter trying her best to be strong, as Dawn was being worked on by the paramedics.

Although Dawn had been revived, her unborn child hadn't survived.

The women felt as if Dawn was being worked on for an eternity. They felt as if the nightmare of their day would never seem to come to an end.

After following behind the paramedics to the hospital, the woman never once thought about reaching out to Dawn's husband Carl.

After getting Dawn through surgery and settled into her room for the night. Dena, Taj, and Amina all decided on staying until Dawn awaken from surgery that night. The three women sat patiently beside Dawn's hospital bed never once thinking about notifying Carl.

Seeing that everything had happened so sudden all four of the woman rushed out of the house without taking their cellphones or personal belongings. Meanwhile, Carl and Dawn's son had been at home worried sick, seeing that it had now been close to midnight and neither one of them heard from Dawn.

Carl began to get impatient, and as he started to panic and become frustrated. He quickly picked up his cellphone for what seemed like the thousandth time to reach out to Taj, Dena, Amina, and his wife Dawn with no response.

"Dad, I just called the hospital, they said that mom was there but they couldn't give me any information. They said that we had to come down there if we wanted to find out anything." Dawn's son informed his step-father Carl while suddenly forming a face full of tears.

Carl hadn't replied to anything that his step-son just said, seeing that he'd been in such a frantic. Instead, Carl quickly grabbed his stepson by the arm leading him out of the front door and towards the car.

The women had all slept inside of Dawn's hospital room while Dawn continued doing the same thing.

"Oh, my god baby! What happened? Are you okay?" Carl suddenly ran into the room questioning Dawn's incoherent body as he kneeled down and held tight to her hand.

Carl swiftly looked up to notice that all three of the women had been balled up on the small sofa on the opposite side of the room.

"So none of you bitches could call me and let me know what in the fuck was going on with my got damn wife and baby!" Carl yelled out to Dena, Taj, and Amina with anger and rage in his voice.

"Dad, calm down, you're going to scare mom." Dawn's son reminded him, scared about everything that'd been going on around him.

Carl looked down at his stepson who been standing directly beside him disappointed with himself. Not only had Carl been disappointed with the way he found out about his wife and unborn child. He'd also been embarrassed with the way he acted in front of his stepson.

Seeing that Carl had been angry with fear and embarrassment, he quickly stormed out of his incoherent wife's hospital room.

"Humph, I'll go talk to him." Taj informed Dena and Amina while swiftly walking out of the room behind him.

"Te Te, is my mom going to be okay, Dawn's son looked up and asked Dena trying his best to fight back his tears.

Dena jumped up from off the small sofa to run over towards her nephew's aid to comfort him. As she wrapped him close in her arms hugging him tightly, seeing that she hadn't known how to feel.

"Your mom's going to be alright baby, just keep praying that God bless us with keeping her here." Dena softly said to her nephew while walking him over toward the small sofa, trying her best to comfort both of their fears.

"Dena, did you call your mom yet and let her know what's going on." Amina questioned her while making room on the small couch for their nephew and them.

"I left out of the house in such a got damn rush, until I left everything except for my got damn house keys. Damn, the only thing I have on me right now Amina is the clothes on my back and a set of keys." Dena looked over and said to her best friend while shaking her head from the disappointment that she's caused upon herself.

"Well, don't beat yourself up about it, just use the hospital phone to let them know what's going on." Amina suggested while pointing towards the nurse's station.

"I brought my phone, y'all can use it to call granny if you want to." Dawn's son interrupted them and suggested while holding out his cellphone towards the both of them.

Dena looked at the phone for what seemed like an eternity before finally deciding on taking it out of her nephew's hands. Once she got the phone, she decided on walking over towards the bathroom so that she could have privacy when speaking with her parents.

"Your mom's going to be alright little man, don't you worry about a thing." Amina assured Dawn's son while tapping him on the nose as if he was a small kid.

"It's not my mom that I'm worried about Te Te, I'm worried about her baby, we were all excited, especially my dad. I don't think she told you guys yet but she was having twins." Dawn's son informed Amina while fidgeting with his fingers and looking towards his mother.

Amina quickly looked at Dawn's son with suspense in her eyes as she hadn't known that Dawn was expecting twins. Seeing that the Doctors hadn't specified if Dawn lost one or two children, Amina had been lost for words.

Amina hadn't known how to react, or what to feel, neither did she have the words to console her nephew. Amina was out of tears, and she felt as if she suddenly lost all of her hope and faith.

Amina knew better than to tell Dawn's son that his mom may have lost both of her twins. Instead, Amina remained quiet, she knew that it wasn't her place to inform him about his mother's condition.

"Twins." Amina whispered to herself as she grasped at her chest confused on why the paramedics hadn't mentioned the death of twins.

"They said that shit as if it was only one baby." Amina silently whispered to herself assuring that no one else was able to hear her.

"Mamma, are you with daddy?" Dena softly questioned her mother over the phone.

After sitting in the restroom for more than ten minutes constipating with herself about how she was going to break the news about Dawn to their parents. Dena stalled the conversation with her mother seeing that she refused on causing her any stress or worries knowing that Dawn was going to be okay.

At first, Dena was hesitant about telling her parents that Dawn had lost her baby, with everyone in the family being excited. Dena didn't know how to break the news.

Not only had Dena went out of her way for Dawn and Carl's wedding, but she also went above and beyond for their new baby.

"What's wrong baby girl." Dena's mother asked her with concern in her voice while placing the phone closer to her ear.

Dena slowly went into detail with her mother explaining what happened with Ayseana before informing her about Dawn.

Dena felt that it would ease her mother's stress about Dawn if she explained to her what lead up to Dawn's tragic incident.

"Well, don't you stress off of Dawn, she's going to be alright. Hell, she doesn't need any more damn kids as it is anyway! Shit, we all know that she doesn't take care of that boy,

as it is. Dena don't you sit up here and act like her so-called husband ain't the reason for having that bastard child live with her tired sorry ass. Shit, that man is a blessing to Dawn and for Dawn! Did they thank you for the wedding by the way?" Dena's mother hastily asked her while resting back in her recliner chair and searching on a small table for her remote control.

"Mamma, stop being so hard on her damn, she needs you right now." Dena whispered over the phone while trying her best to empathize with her mother's pitty.

"Girl shut your little bougie ass the fuck up! I ain't trying to hear that sentimental ass bullshit about your got damn sister right now! Your sister ain't shit, did you seem to forget Dena, she's the reason for your bitterness. Don't act like Dawn ain't do you no mother fucking favor by fucking on that criminal ass ex-boyfriend of yours. Did you suddenly forget about your retarded ass nephew they made for you? I'm not the one Dena, God forgives, but baby, your mother doesn't! I raised you mother fucking girls way better than that. Your father and I worked hard to show you the example of a successful black family. And look at what this little hoe ass bitch go out and do. Don't think they ain't talk about y'all down at the church." Dena's mother nonchalantly and sarcastically reminded her over the phone while now inhaling the smoke from

her Newport cigarette.

"Mamma! I can't believe you right now, this isn't the time to be petty! What in the hell is wrong with you? Mamma, you straight up tripping, who talks like that about their own child and grandson." Dena whined to her mother over the phone while holding back her tears and unwanted bickering.

"Dena, Dena, Dena I can give two fucks about how you feel about the whole mother fucking situation. Bitch I'm your mother fucking mother, your not mine. Don't you sit you little narrow ass up here on this phone and tell me a got damn thing about nothing that I spit out of my pussy! Do you understand me, little girl? You know it and I no it, hell the whole mother fucking world probably no of it, Dawn's bitch ass ain't shit! I birthed a slut! Yea, her mother fucking mamma said it, you probably ain't tripping, but baby girl, yo mamma been tripping. Ask the little bitch why I put her ass OUT! Dena, I don't play that shit, karma is a bitch, and she was hard on me for no reason. If it wasn't for you being the mature younger sister, shit, Dawn's ignorant little dumb ass would probably be somewhere dead. You know she got that dog ass shit from ya daddy and nem side. That's exactly how yo aunt Pam did ya, auntie Gina!" Dena's mom went on to say while rambling on and on, with no consideration for Dawn's situation.

Dena didn't know how to react, nor did she know how to respond to her mother's reactions about her feeling towards her own daughter.

"Really mamma, I truly can't believe you right now! Imma call you back later, I have to look out for Dawn since you not willing to." Dena coldly said to her mother before getting ready to disconnect their call.

"Like I said, I can give two fucks about how you feel Dena, call me when the bitch is dead if it's that serious!" Dena's mom rudely said before taking another puff of her cigarette and closing her small flip phone in Dena's ear.

"Hello, hello mom. I no mother fucking well this old miserable bitch ain't just hang up in my face." Dena said to herself while clinching on her teeth with frustration and anger.

Dena got up from the toilet top that she'd been sitting on while on the phone with her mother to walk back into Dawn's hospital room.

Dena walked out of the bathroom towards the side of Dawn's hospital bed with a blank look on her face as she tried her best to fight back her tears. She softly rubbed on her older sister's faces as she took the same hand to softly brush her hair back from falling in front of her face.

After leaning over Dawn for a few seconds, Dena leaned in to softly kiss her on the forehead. After checking up on Dawn, Dena looked over at Amina and Dawn's son as she walked out of the hospital room to join Carl and Taj.

Taj and Carl had been coming back from the hospital break room when they bumped into Dena searching for them in the hallway. The trio stood in the hallway for about thirty more minutes talking amongst each other before joining everyone back in Dawn's hospital room.

Although Dena's mother hadn't given them the response that she wanted about her older sister. Dena decided on keeping her mothers condolence and comments to herself.

After feeling Amina in about the twins that Dawn and Carl were expecting, everyone begin to have different emotions and mixed feelings.

The group remained at the hospital with Dawn and her family late into the night, before deciding with each other that it had been time for them to leave.

Dena, Taj, and Amina later found out that both of the twins passed away on their ride home. Carl, Dawn, and her son decided on staying behind at the hospital until it was time for Dawn to be discharged.

Seeing that everything happened so vastly, no one had time to take in Ayseana suicide, nor had they come to realize her death as a reality.

The girls sat in silence as they carpooled on the eight eighty freeway headed in various directions home.

"You want us to come over and help you straighten up the house." Taj softly asked Dena trying her best to break the unwanted miserable silence that filled the small SUV.

Although Dena heard exactly what Taj asked her, she took a moment to respond.

"Nah, I'm good, that's why I have my cleaning staff. I wish that I would come home to a filthy house! My mother fucking shit better look like nothing ever fucking happened at all today!" Dena sarcastically said to Taj while glancing over at Amina in the back seat.

Once Dena got home late that night, Taj and Amina quickly hopped into their cars, as Dena slowly made her way inside. Once inside of her house, Dena had finally been able to grasp a hold of herself well as her thoughts and feelings.

Although Taj and Amina were more like family than best friends to Dena. Dena comes to realize with herself that she needed time away from everyone else.

Now that Dena was safely tucked in the comfort of her bed late that night. Dena concludes with herself that she needed to focus on herself.

Taj hadn't known how to feel the next morning seeing that her emotions were everywhere outside of her main focus.

Amina on the other hand went inside of her apartment only to grab a few of her things to take life's reality to the streets of San Francisco.

Earlier that day so much had happened to the group of women within a twenty-four-hour period.

With Dawn's situation happening in their presence, none of the girls seemed to remember Ayseana death.

Days turned into weeks, as weeks turned into months. It had now been close towards the holiday season when Dena decided with herself that she'd invite the girls and her family over for Christmas dinner.

Seeing that Dena abandoned her friends and family during Dawn's tragic incident, their communication seemed odd once she decided on reaching back out to them. With no one reaching back out to Dena, things quickly change about her plans for dinner that holiday.

With Dena growing accustomed to being alone, she purposely avoided all contact and communication with her family and friends.

Dena's disagreement with her mother's attitude toward Dawn made her decided on cutting her parents completely off. She was so upset with her mother until she refused on supporting them any further. Not only had Dena cut off her parents, but she'd also cut off all of her siblings, including her older sister Dawn.

Dena's mother had opened up old wounds that Dena tried desperately to forget and hide. With Dawn breaking Dena's heart by taking her first love. Dena refused on supporting Dawn and her son any further.

Although Taj and Amina hadn't had anything to do with Dena's heartbreak and frustration, Dena decided on cutting them off as well.

With Taj and Amina growing frustrated with trying to reach out to Dena, they too became distant friends that once were close.

Unbeknownst to Dena, she distracted their friendship and broken up everyone's tight nit bond. With Dena being the peacemaker of the group, the girls had no one to orchestrated their friendship.

Seeing that Dena secluded herself the friendship that the girls tried so hard to desperately hold tight to, no longer existed.

.

Books By:
Author Black Barbie

Skeemin On Tha Low
Skeemin On Tha Low 2
The War On Us
Inspire 2B Inspired
What Is Love
RICHMOND
FRIENDS

Coming 2021

Hoes UP ~ Pimp's Down

Website: www.authorblackbarbie.com
Email: authorblackbarbie@gmail.com